"Don't you like men?" Niall asked dryly

"They have their uses," replied Susanna coolly, "but I'm not in the market for one at the moment. Even if I were, I certainly wouldn't pick you."

"Charm isn't your strong point, is it?"

"Where you're concerned, no. I wouldn't want it to be."

His face took on an angry color that Susanna was secretly relieved to see. Hostility was safer than the other emotions that flowed between them.

"You don't wrap things up, do you?" Niall muttered, watching her oddly. "You call it as you see it. Nobody could accuse you of being deceptive; you don't hide a thing."

Don't I? she thought, distinctly worried by that remark. She didn't want this man guessing things about her. There were too many feelings she didn't understand herself that she didn't want him to know.

Books by Charlotte Lamb

A VIOLATION

HARLEQUIN PRESENTS

HARLEQUIN ROMANCE

These books may be available at your local bookseller.

Don't miss any of our special offers. Write to us at the following address for information on our newest releases.

Harlequin Reader Service
P.O. Box 52040, Phoenix, AZ   85072-2040
Canadian address: P.O. Box 2800, Postal Station A,
5170 Yonge St., Willowdale, Ont.   M2N 6J3

CHARLOTTE LAMB

for adults only

Harlequin Books

TORONTO • NEW YORK • LONDON
AMSTERDAM • PARIS • SYDNEY • HAMBURG
STOCKHOLM • ATHENS • TOKYO • MILAN

Harlequin Presents first edition February 1985
ISBN 0-373-10762-5

Original hardcover edition published in 1984
by Mills & Boon Limited

CHAPTER ONE

A BLUEBOTTLE must have got into the bedroom, in spite of the hermetically sealed double-glazing. It was buzzing around Susanna's ear like a helicopter looking for a landing pad. She flapped a hand to drive it away, but the thing was persistent, the buzzing did not stop, and Susanna suddenly realised that it wasn't an insect at all. The doorbell was ringing.

Fumbling for the alarm clock she peered at it through half-closed eyes. Nine o'clock. Her eyes opened fully.

'Oh, no! I've overslept!' She stumbled out of the bed in panic and snatched up a pink silk robe. While she was sliding her arms into it and tying the wide belt, the bell continued to ring and she opened her bedroom door to yell down the corridor.

'Okay, okay, I'm coming!'

Who on earth could it be? She paused to look at herself in the dressing-table mirror, grimacing. Surely Johnny had not arrived this early?

'What do you look like?' she asked her reflection ruefully as she ran a comb through her tousled brown hair. Her face was flushed with sleep, her eyes still drowsy, the silk robe clung to her bedwarm body, but she did not have time to do anything much about the way she looked. That damned bell was still ringing.

She pulled open the door and the man who had

been leaning on her bell scowled down at her. He had a long way to scowl; he was over six foot and Susanna was scarcely five foot three in her bare feet, a difference of which she was immediately conscious.

'Susanna Howard?'

'Yes, and please take your thumb off my bell, you're giving me a headache.' She watched him lift his hand, slowly. She had never seen him before, she was certain of that, but she knew three things about him already—he was too big, he was a very angry man and she did not like him. He had the sort of face that threatens without moving a muscle.

'What do you want?' she asked, clutching the neck of her robe as he made a thorough survey of her with narrowed grey eyes which clearly did not think much of what they saw. Remembering how she had looked in the mirror a moment ago, Susanna could not really blame him for the lifted eyebrows, but the contemptuous twist of his mouth made her furious.

'I'm Niall Ardrey,' he said and she stared at him blankly. The name meant nothing to her.

'Don't pretend you've never heard of me!'

'I wasn't pretending, I haven't. What can I do for you, Mr Ard. . . .'

He spelt his name in a slow distinct voice, like someone talking to an idiot while Susanna wondered if she should have left the chain on the door before she was silly enough to open it. Probably she should have done; but then who expects to open the door, on a peaceful Sunday morning, to a guy who looks like the Incredible Hulk?

'I've come for my sister,' he said. He was not talking to Susanna, she suddenly realised, he was carefully projecting his voice into the furthest recesses of her flat. 'I know she's here and I'm not leaving without her.'

'I don't know what you're talking about!' Susanna had begun to wonder what she would do if he turned out to be as dangerous as he looked. She could always scream, of course—supposing that he gave her the chance. Somehow, though, she got the feeling that he wasn't likely to do that. For all his height and muscle, she sensed that he was quick on his feet; he had a loose-limbed ease of movement which in a less powerful man you might call grace.

'Don't play games with me, Miss Howard!' he said impatiently, scowling. His eyebrows were black and heavy, scowling was a natural expression to them.

'I wasn't intending to!' Susanna said with dry emphasis. 'Are you sure you've got the right name and address? What's your sister's name?'

'Sîan. Sîan Ardrey,' he said through tight lips. 'I haven't got time for all this. I know she's here— and she might as well come out now from wherever she's hiding because I intend to search this flat until I've found her.'

'You aren't searching my flat!' Susanna said, moving sideways to block him as he seemed about to push his way into the flat. 'I've never even heard of your sister. What's this all about?'

'You don't know, of course,' he said with angry mockery, his mouth twisting. 'You're doing a very good job of acting wide-eyed and innocent, Miss Howard, but it won't wash. I don't fall for that sort of routine any more. I stopped believing in fairies when I was five years old.'

'I'm sure you were very precocious,' Susanna said bitingly. 'But I assure you I'm not acting. You've made a mistake and I advise you to go back to square one and start looking for your sister somewhere else. You won't find her here. I don't know how you got the impression that I knew her or that she was with me, but. . . .'

'Your brother's flatmate told me.'

Susanna's face changed, her eyes suddenly sharp and attentive. 'Ian?'

'Yes. I see you're taking me seriously at last.' Niall Ardrey's mouth was ironic. 'Your brother's flatmate didn't want to tell me. Like you, he started out by lying his head off, but I persuaded him to tell me the truth, in the end.'

'You persuaded him?' Susanna said slowly, her mind busy wondering how her brother was mixed up in this while her brown eyes wandered up and down the formidable man facing her, from his thick black hair to his long legs.

He nodded and looking into his hard grey eyes she could easily imagine the sort of persuasion he had used.

'Poor Ian—which ward is he in?'

'Very witty,' he said with no visible sign of amusement. 'Now, are you going to let me see Sîan or am I going to have to do this the hard way?'

'I've told you, I don't even know your sister. I'm alone here.' Susanna stopped abruptly, her face uneasy—maybe it hadn't been a good idea to admit that she was alone in the flat. She didn't like that look in his eyes, it was making the back of her neck prickle with a sense of danger. Hurriedly she began to close the door but Niall Ardrey leant on it and forced it open again. Susanna was flung backwards with it and reeled against the wall. The next minute she saw his back as he vanished down the corridor, his stride carrying him forward too fast for her to catch him.

'What do you think you're doing? Get out of my flat! How dare you force your way in here like this?' Susanna ran after him, flushed and incredulous, unable to believe that this was happening to her. He was in her bedroom by the time she reached his side and her face was hot as she saw him glancing around, eying the tumbled bed from which she had so recently risen. He ignored her protests, walking over to the wardrobe and pushing aside the rows of clothes hanging in it, to peer behind them. To her disbelief he even bent down and looked under her bed.

Bristling, Susanna said: 'I'm going to ring the police if you aren't out of my flat in one minute!'

Niall Ardrey turned towards her and walked out of the bedroom door, but he did not leave. He went into the bathroom, she heard him pulling back the shower curtain.

Susanna ran back down the corridor to her sitting room and snatched up the phone. She began to dial, her fingers trembling. A hand came over her shoulder, took the receiver from her before she could tighten her hold on it, and replaced it.

Clutching the lapels of her robe together to hide the glimpse of her breasts he might otherwise have had, Susanna turned nervously and faced him.

'Where is she?' he demanded.

'I told you—I don't even know your sister, I've

never heard of her. I've never heard of you. I wish I hadn't heard of you now. I have no idea what this is all about, but you have no right to force your way into my flat and start searching it.' She almost gabbled the words in a breathless, unsteady voice. She was shaking but her chin was lifted defiantly, her brown eyes shifted sideways to search for some weapon she could grab. There was a brass candlestick on the mantelpiece. That might do, it was certainly heavy enough. If she could just edge her way towards it she could pick it up before he realised what was in her mind.

His hard eyes followed the direction of her glance. 'Oh, no, you don't,' he said drily and his hands shot out to grasp her waist. Susanna gave a gasp of shock. He lifted her effortlessly, she felt her feet leave the ground and struggled, flailing at him with both hands. Ignoring her slaps he carried her over to the couch and dropped her on it. He stood over her menacingly, his feet apart, his body looming. Susanna stared up at him, nervously aware that they were alone and she was very skimpily dressed.

Her thin robe covered but did not hide the fragile, transparent nightdress under it; her smooth bare skin showed through both and she was agitated under Niall Ardrey's observant scrutiny. What was he thinking about as his eyes moved over her? Susanna was glad she didn't know; what she guessed was worrying enough. She held her robe together at the throat, huddling back on the couch, waiting for a chance to get away from him and trying to remember the right way to fight back if you were attacked. Should she scream now or would that just precipitate the worst?

'Miss Howard,' he said in a voice which seemed cool and rational enough. 'My sister is seventeen years old. She only left school five weeks ago and in the autumn she will be going up to university. I won't allow her—or anyone else, come to that—to ruin her future. She isn't marrying your brother. . . .'

'Marrying?' Susanna interrupted sharply, incredulously, hardly believing her ears, and sitting up again, forgetting her fear for herself.

He stared at her, his mouth hard. 'Hadn't they told you?'

'Alex? Your sister wants to marry Alex?'

His black brows jerked together. 'You have that the wrong way round. Your brother plans to run off with my sister and marry her. He's a shrewd, ambitious young man, your brother; but he isn't getting away with it. My plans for my sister don't involve a disastrous marriage to someone like him.'

Susanna's eyes flashed, their usual warmth darkening with anger. 'Do you *know* my brother?' She bitterly resented the way he had talked about Alex.

'I know all about him. I spent yesterday finding out everything I could; I had a private detective hunting up every detail of his life and it was hardly reassuring. He doesn't have any money and he's had three different jobs in the last two years. He'll be looking for another one soon. He isn't working for me any more.'

'Working for you? What are you talking about? Alex doesn't work for you. I've met his boss, he works for a man called Houghton and you don't look anything like him.' Susanna was beginning to feel she had wandered into a madhouse and Niall Ardrey was one of the inhabitants, nothing he had said to her so far made sense.

'I know where he works,' Niall Ardrey said with an impatient shrug and a stare which held distinct irritation. 'Houghton, Elks and Wilmer,' he added as she opened her mouth to ask where he *thought* Alex worked, and Susanna shut her mouth again, frowning. He had got that right, anyway.

She had been deeply relieved when Alex got a job in the large advertising agency which had offices in a narrow lane off Bond Street. Alex had drifted from job to job since he left school. He was never fired, he always resigned because he found the work boring, and he had never seemed to have much trouble getting another job but Susanna had been worried by what had begun to look like a pattern. With so much unemployment in the country Alex could not rely on always being able to get another job. He had been lucky so far; he was quick and intelligent and most people liked him on sight, but his employment record made him a risk. Susanna had been delighted when it seemed that Alex was settling down happily in the advertising agency. He enjoyed what he was doing, he was interested in the work and he liked his new boss, he told her. It had been a weight off her shoulders.

She did not mind lending him money while he was between jobs and his flatmate, Ian, an old schoolfriend with a steady job at which he was doing well, seemed cheerful about paying the rent for both of them until Alex could come up with his share. Alex always paid them both back; he was not extravagant and he did not enjoy owing money. Susanna's only anxiety was about Alex himself; when he was restless and dissatisfied it made Susanna uneasy.

'Do you work in the agency, then? What do you do?' she asked Niall Ardrey whose mouth compressed. He gave her a cynical smile, those eyebrows lifting again.

'Oh, of course, you don't know who I am.' He clearly did not believe her and Susanna was furious, her face becoming heated.

'I'm getting pretty sick of telling you that I've never even heard of you!'

'And I'm getting pretty sick of pretending to believe you!' he retorted. 'But since you insist on going through this ludicrous charade—I don't work at Houghton, Elks and Wilmer. I haven't got time to explain all the ramifications of my business, but I control the holding company which controls Houghton, Elks and Wilmer.' He was talking in a slow, distinct, sardonic voice meant to be offensive and Susanna was more than ready to take offence. 'Of course you didn't know that, you don't know that my sister is a considerable heiress and will one day be a very rich woman.'

Susanna stared back at him, for the first time noticing the expensive tailoring of his dark grey striped suit. His jacket was open; she could see the smooth-fitting waistcoat under it and below that a dark-striped shirt and a wine-coloured silk tie. He was far from being elegant; his body had too much power, was too forceful and muscular. It was his innately threatening presence that she had noticed until now, but as she studied him she realised that he must be very wealthy. That suit probably cost more than she spent on clothes in a year.

She shrugged resentfully. 'You don't know my brother or you wouldn't suspect that money would mean a thing to him. Alex isn't a fortune-hunter.'

'Wouldn't it?' Niall Ardrey smiled drily. 'Don't try to con me, Miss Howard, because better women than you have tried and failed. I don't intend to get involved in argument with you. I just want my sister back unharmed. . . .'

'Unharmed?' Susanna repeated, interrupting, and going pale. 'What do you mean by that?'

'We're both adults! You know exactly what I mean by that. Sîan has spent the past eight years in a very strict boarding school. Her only contact with boys was at the monthly school dance, which was carefully supervised, and her partners were all from a nearby boys' boarding school. Even then she was never left alone with any of them; the staff made sure of that. Sîan is totally inexperienced.'

Susanna's eyes were angry as she thought about the implications of what he had been saying. She stared at him, trembling.

'If she's as innocent as you claim, she won't come to any harm with my brother. Alex is a very nice boy, he's only had a couple of girlfriends himself. He's not some smooth-talking seducer with an eye to the main chance. That's what you think, isn't it? That he's been chasing your sister because she will inherit a lot of money?'

'What do you expect me to think?' Niall Ardrey enquired coldly. 'He has run off with Sîan. She wrote to me and told me she was going to marry him. I suppose they thought I wouldn't get the letter for days and by the time I did get it, it would be too late for me to do anything about it, but luckily I arrived in London yesterday unexpectedly and instead of being sent off to New York to me, I got the letter the day it arrived. I went round to the flat where Sîan had been staying and it was empty. I discovered that the family I left her with had gone away for a few days, leaving her there alone. When I managed to get in touch with them in the Lake District they didn't know where she was, thought she was in the London flat.' His face darkened. 'I had trusted them to look after her, it never occurred to me that they would go away leaving her on her own.' Susanna was sorry for them, whoever they were. It must have been a fraught conversation, no doubt Niall Ardrey had been cutting. That little chat would have ruined their holiday.

'Are you sure it's Alex she has run off with? How did she meet him?'

'At the advertising agency, obviously,' Niall Ardrey said impatiently. 'She wanted to work during her summer holiday and I approved of the idea.' He caught Susanna's eyes and stopped, his brows jerking together in a straight black line. 'Why are you looking at me like that?' he demanded and she gave him a bland smile.

'Oh, nothing, I was just so surprised to hear that you approved of anything.'

'I don't find you in the least amusing, Miss Howard,' he informed her and went on. 'I got Sîan part-time work in the advertising agency, asked these relatives to look after her as they had a daughter of the same age and I thought it would be good for Sîan to have company of her own age, then I flew to New York on urgent business. I've only been away for three weeks. Your brother must have worked fast.'

'Or your sister did,' Susanna added softly and he eyed her with distaste.

'Sîan is still a child.'

'What do you think Alex is? He's twenty-two, Mr Ardrey. I know him better than anyone else in the world. You don't have to worry about your sister if she's with Alex and I'm still not convinced that she is . . . may I see this letter she left?'

She was surprised when a faint dark red crept into his face. 'No,' he said tersely. 'You may not. It is private, but I assure you that she says she is going away with your brother and is going to marry him.'

'Is he her first boyfriend?' Susanna asked slowly, thinking hard. 'Yes, of course, he must be. Doesn't it seem a little odd to you? I mean, running away with the first boy she meets, talking about marrying him after knowing him for just a few weeks? Why didn't she introduce Alex to you? Why isn't she dating him and getting to know him? Why all the drama and secrecy?'

'No doubt she took your brother's advice,' Niall Ardrey said sharply. 'His flatmate admitted that they were together. He said they had come to you.' He bent towards her, his grey eyes icy. 'Which is where we came in . . . tell me where they are, because if Sîan isn't safely back with me tonight I am going to the police. She's under age, she won't be eighteen for several months. She must have my permission before she can get married.'

'I don't know where they are,' Susanna insisted, her body rigid under the threat of his proximity.

He stared down into her face for a moment without speaking, then straightened. 'Just as you like, but if you're wise you'll give your brother my message. Either Sîan comes home tonight or I contact the police. There's one aspect he may not have realised—Sîan doesn't inherit her money until she's twenty-five. Under her grandfather's will three executors control the trust fund until that time. I am one of them and the other two will agree with any decision I make. I can release Sîan's income from the trust at my discretion. Your brother might as well know that I won't part with a penny of that fund if she marries him. They'll have to wait seven years for the money.' He turned on his heel without waiting for any reaction from Susanna and walked out of the flat while she sat on the couch, so angry she was shaking.

When she heard the slam of the front door she got up and unsteadily made her way to the bathroom. She showered and dressed in jeans and a yellow silk shirt, made some coffee and toast and when she had had a rapid breakfast went to ring her own boyfriend. She had planned to spend that Sunday with Johnny, they had been going into the country to have lunch at a quiet pub he knew.

Johnny sounded amused when he heard her voice. 'Don't tell me! You forgot we were going out and slept through your alarm? Typical, I knew you would.'

'No, it isn't that, Johnny.' Susanna unconsciously relaxed as she heard his smiling voice. Johnny always had that effect on her; he was a lively, warm-hearted man who did not take anything very seriously and did not want anyone to take him seriously, either. Susanna's friends had warned her off him when they heard that she was dating Johnny. He can't be relied on, he isn't the serious type, don't get involved with him or you might get hurt, they had said over and over again. Susanna had shrugged off their warnings. She didn't want to find a husband, she was far too busy and she enjoyed her job too much. She wanted a friend, a playmate, perhaps—and Johnny was perfect for that role, it was type-casting.

'I'm afraid I can't come today. I have to go down to the cottage to see Alex,' she said, glancing at her watch. 'I can't stop, I'm going to have to rush. I'm sorry, Johnny. I'll take *you* somewhere next week, okay?'

'Hang on, hang on—why are you going down to the cottage to see Alex? Anything wrong?'

'I don't know, I'm going down there to see.'

'You're very cryptic this morning. Is Alex in trouble?'

'I hope not.'

'Can I come along? Or will I be in the way?'

Susanna hesitated, biting her lower lip as she considered that. 'I think you'd better not,' she said after a pause. 'Alex might prefer it if I came alone. This is family business.'

'Oh, dear,' Johnny said teasingly. 'Poor Alex; is he going to get spanked?'

'Idiot. See you, have a nice day and I'm sorry to miss it.' Susanna hung up and went into the bathroom to brush her hair and put on some make-up. She had never been a beautiful girl but with a little expertise she could make herself look attractive enough to get second looks from men. Her brown hair had rich red highlights in it and curled softly around her face, her eyes were large and lustrous. A romantic young man had once told her she had eyes like a doe and had looked hurt when Susanna laughed.

Susanna was not romantic; she was down to earth and practical, vividly alive and funny in some moods but essentially level-headed. Her sense of humour would never let her take life too seriously, which was probably why she got on so well with Johnny. They amused each other and had fun doing it but neither of them imagined that they were in love. Susanna was not even sure she knew what people meant when they talked about being in love. She had never been in love. She had had the measles, she had broken an arm falling out of a tree as a child, she had spent a whole year once collecting pictures of a favourite pop star, but she had never felt her heart turn over and she did not believe hearts did so. She had never stayed awake thinking about any of the boys she dated although she enjoyed being kissed and liked it when someone whistled after her in the street. She understood sex, she wanted one day to get married, and when she decided on the right man she was sure she would be happy with him, but she did not expect to see stars every time he smiled at her or walk on air because he held her hand.

She had discovered long ago that the opposite sex cannot take being laughed at; nothing killed a romantic mood faster than a well-timed giggle. Susanna's sense of humour wouldn't allow her to ignore the ridiculous and she found love faintly absurd. What was worrying her at the moment was that her brother did not share her view of romance. Alex had always been susceptible, idealistic, full of dreams. If he really had fallen in love with Niall Ardrey's little sister Susanna saw dangers ahead.

She slipped on a lightweight wool jacket and left

her flat a moment later. Her car was parked in the communal garage in the basement of the building which held shops and offices as well as flats. Susanna earned a very good salary as a commercial artist. Since she had left art college she had been in work continuously; designing book jackets, doing magazine art and illustrating books. The rent of her flat was rather high but it was quite central, she could get to any part of London quickly from there. Her car was a small blue Ford; three years old but still reliable and would, she hoped, continue to run without trouble for a few years yet.

She headed out of town towards Sussex and found the roads choked with traffic. There was no three-lane motorway and a lot of other people had headed for the Sussex coast that day. The journey took even longer than she had anticipated.

As the morning wore on the sun rose high in the sky, the heat uncomfortable. Susanna fished in the glove compartment for a pair of sunglasses and slipped them on to lessen the glare. She always got a headache when she drove in bright sunshine, especially on crowded roads; jerking and edging forward a few inches at a time, forced to concentrate on the road ahead so that her eyes screwed up and her forehead was wrinkled.

Where else could Alex have taken Sîan Ardrey but the cottage? That must have been what Ian had meant when he told Niall Ardrey that they had gone to stay with Susanna. Legally the cottage was her property, although Susanna saw it as Alex's home, too. After all, it had always been their home, they had both been born there. When their mother died she left the cottage to Susanna and most of the money she had for Alex. When she made her will Alex had only been a boy of fifteen; she must have made it shortly after her husband's death. She had left all the money in a trust fund. Alex received it when he married. It was no great sum, nothing to compare with the money Sîan Ardrey would no doubt inherit one day. It was by now around five thousand pounds, though, and would make a useful deposit on a house when Alex married.

When the family lawyer read them the will, Susanna had been taken aback. 'Why did she leave the cottage to me, not to Alex? Or to both of us? It seems very unfair. The cottage must be worth at least thirty thousand.'

'Twenty-five at most,' the lawyer had said. Susanna had shrugged.

'All the same, I shall sell it and divide the money with you, Alex—it's the only fair thing to do.'

'I don't want you to sell it,' Alex had said at once and the lawyer had chimed in: 'Your mother didn't want the cottage sold.' They both looked at him and he added: 'She wanted it to remain your family home for as long as possible, and she thought perhaps one day one of you would want to live in it when you married.' He had smiled at them paternally, his white head nodding. 'Your mother had a romantic streak.'

'I agree with Mum,' Alex said firmly. 'I'd hate to see strangers in the old place and it would be wonderful to be able to come here at weekends and Christmas and for summer holidays. Okay, we both work in London at the moment, but who knows? I vote you keep it, Susie.'

'Don't call me Susie,' she had said automatically,

hating her old childhood nickname, but she had accepted Alex's decision, especially after a talk she had alone with the lawyer later when he told her that their mother had been worried about Alex's restless inability to settle to anything and had been afraid that if he had a large sum of money he would spend it all and end up with nothing.

'If the cottage is there, he'll always have a home, at least,' the lawyer had added. 'That was why your mother left it to you, not him. I suggested altering the will many times but she refused. She felt Alex was too unstable. She was sure you would always take care of him, so she left the place to you.'

Susanna had nodded slowly. 'She had a point. Okay, I keep it for the moment and we'll see what happens. Alex may need money one day.'

It was almost two years since their mother died and they had visited the cottage frequently during that time; together or alone or with friends. Occasionally they had rented the place to friends. Susanna had always insisted on splitting the rent with Alex who always argued vehemently over it. 'Pay the rates with it, pay the heating bills and the cleaning woman. I don't want it,' he always said. Susanna usually found a way of handing it on to him which his pride would permit. Alex would borrow money from her, but he would not take it unless he could pay it back. He would accept a pair of gloves or a bottle of wine but if they went to the cinema he wouldn't let Susanna pay for his ticket. If they went out to dinner he insisted on paying for himself if not for her. Alex resented having to ask her for help when he was in trouble, yet he always came and Susanna always gave him

help, knowing very well that her brother would
have given anything to be the one who gave, not
the one who received. Their relationship was
close and loving and as prickly as a nest full of
hedgehogs. At times she wondered if Alex would
have been very different if he had been the elder.
She suspected that he resented her three years
seniority. He hated being her little brother, but
that was what he would always be for the rest of
their lives.

It was lunchtime as she drove up the narrow,
winding lane which led to the cottage. The hedges
were in full leaf, noisy with birds and brilliant with
wild flowers blowing beneath them; chicory and
willowherb and blue bugloss, big pink thistles and
yellow St John's wort, all the old familiar flowers
she remembered from childhood summers. The
cottage was hidden away behind ancient, high
privet hedges in which robins nested in the spring
and which in high summer were decked with white
flowers which smelt pungently after rain.

Susanna's pleasure in revisiting old haunts was
somewhat spoiled, however, because she was
rather worried about a car which was following
her own, not too close; at a respectful distance but
never losing sight of her. She had first become
aware of it some miles back, when she turned off
the main Brighton road. She might not have
noticed it even then if the driver had not suddenly
braked with a screeching noise and turned sharply
to follow her, almost crashing with the car behind
him which responded by a prolonged blare of the
horn. Susanna had looked back curiously as she
drove on, noticing the beige saloon and catching
sight of the number plate. It made her smile

because the letters on it spelt MAD. From time to time as she turned a corner she would become aware of the car again. It kept a position far enough behind her not to be too obvious, but although she was taking a complicated cross-country route to a remote village the car behind stayed on her trail.

It seemed crazy, it might be pure coincidence, but Susanna kept looking back in alarm. She was sure the car was following her now. Which could only mean one thing—that the driver was hoping she would lead him somewhere. To her brother and Sîan Ardrey?

It had to be Niall Ardrey in that car. What should she do about it? She slowed down, thinking furiously. A corner was just up ahead. Susanna knew she was only two minutes away from the cottage, she had to get rid of her pursuer before she got there. She took the corner and as soon as she was out of sight of the following car she braked sharply to a full stop. A moment later the other car came round the corner and saw her car parked in the verge just too late to stop. Susanna watched with satisfaction as the other car swerved wildly, and drove past. The driver turned his head to glare at her and her body stiffened in shock.

CHAPTER TWO

SHE had been letting her imagination run away with her. The man in the car was not Niall Ardrey at all. He was a middle-aged man with grey hair; wearing a shabby old tweed jacket repaired at the elbows with leather, and he was very angry. He had braked and wound down his window, leaning out to yell insults and comments on her idea of safety on the road. Susanna could not catch everything he said but she got the general idea and blushed, making apologetic gestures at him, feeling very stupid.

'Could have killed me! Women drivers! Shouldn't be allowed behind a wheel! If you were my daughter. . . .'

With a final shake of his fist he drove on at last, leaving Susanna to pull herself together and follow him. She was very cross with herself for letting suspicion addle her brains.

The cottage lay at the very end of the lane, just where it joined another road crossing it in a T-junction. Susanna parked close to the hedge. As she got out of the car she knew her guesswork had been accurate on one point, anyway. Alex was here, and he was not alone. Susanna could not see him or his companion, but she could hear them through the thick hedge. They seemed to be very happy, their voices full of laughter.

Susanna stood, listening, reluctant to go into the garden and put an end to their happiness. She could not help envying them. They sounded as though life was very good; scampering about on the grass like children, rustling through bushes, calling and laughing. From the sound of it they were playing hide-and-seek—hardly a sophisticated game or one even Niall Ardrey could call depraved, but they were obviously having fun and loving every minute of it. Did she have to walk through the gate and ruin the day for them?

She argued with herself, half inclined to get back into the car and drive away. It was none of her business, after all. Her brother was twenty-two years old, he was not her responsibility, and the fact that he had not told her anything about Sîan Ardrey argued that he did not want her involved. In a way that hurt; she and Alex had always been so close, they had not had secrets from each other before. At the same time, Alex was entitled to privacy, she had no right to interfere in his life.

Biting her lip, she remembered Niall Ardrey's angry face and his final threat. What if he did go to the police? What if he did get Alex fired? Susanna had only met Niall Ardrey very briefly, but she had a sinking feeling that he was not a man who made idle threats.

Before she could decide what to do the gate creaked open and she heard running feet. Someone dashed out of the garden; a girl in white jeans and a pink sweatshirt, her long black hair whipped around her face, windblown and dishevelled. She was glancing over her shoulder, laughing. She had not seen Susanna. The next minute Alex shot through the gate and saw Susanna immediately, halting in his tracks. The dark-haired girl skidded to a stop just in time to avoid a collision and stared at Susanna with startled eyes.

'Hallo, Alex,' Susanna said as calmly as she could, watching with regret as the laughter drained out of his thin face and a frown took its place.

'What are you doing here? I thought you were seeing Johnny this weekend? Is he with you?' Alex's dark eyes searched the empty car.

'No, I'm alone.' Susanna glanced at the dark-haired girl who was standing like a statue, listening. She looked so young; Susanna could scarcely believe that she was almost eighteen. She had the slight build and uncertain look of a child, a particularly shy child, her eyes lowered and her slender body tense as though she wanted to run away.

Alex crossed to join her and slid an arm round her waist, his attitude protective. 'This is Sîan,' he said almost belligerently. 'Sîan, my sister, Susanna.'

Susanna smiled as the other girl looked up shyly. 'Hallo, Sîan.' She held out her hand and Sîan took it after a hesitant struggle with herself. Her fingers were tiny and very cold, they trembled slightly.

'Have you had lunch yet? I'm starving. I was going to get something out of the deep freeze. I left it well-stocked last time I came down,' Susanna said.

'We brought chicken and salad. There's enough for you if you'd like that.' Alex turned back into the garden, steering Sîan along with him. Susanna followed them, watching their entwined bodies sympathetically. As if aware of her eyes, Sîan moved closer to Alex, whose arm tightened around her waist, in silent comfort.

The garden was looking lovely; Alex had mowed the lawn and the scent of newly cut grass was nostalgic, reminding Susanna of other summers. The roses were in full bloom, velvety red and smooth white, great open-hearted flowers drenching the air with their perfume and luring the fat goldy bumble bees whose drowsy sound filled the garden. Their long absences during the months of growth had meant that the flower beds were choked with weeds and grass grew between the cracks in the paving, but it did not matter. Summer rose above all that; sending tendrils of sweetpea twining up a trellis, starring the long rough grass with daisies and golden celandine, startling the eye with splashes of crimson poppies and blue scabious.

The cottage was small and gabled, painted green and white, with pink roses growing up the side of the front door and lurching out from the wall to nod sleepily and shower petals on the path. Susanna noted how cracked and peeling the paintwork was, she saw the odd tile missing from the red roof, probably during winter storms, and she thought for the twentieth time that she really must have something done about the state of the place.

'We might as well have lunch now,' Alex said as he pushed open the front door. 'I had to oil the hinges, by the way—they were creaking badly. There's a leak in the attic, too, and ants in the kitchen. We bought some ant powder and put it down. They were everywhere; in the cupboards and on the floor, climbing the walls. We tracked them back to their entry point and I think the nest is under the house.'

Susanna walked into the kitchen and looked around. It was very neat, nothing out of place. It had been left exactly as it had been during their mother's lifetime; a small square room with a white-enamelled kitchen range taking up a lot of space on one wall and a scrubbed deal table in the centre of the room. The kitchen cabinets were quite old, but their mother had painted them a sunny yellow which disguised their age, and made the kitchen a welcoming place especially in the early morning on a wintry day.

'Before we have lunch I've got to talk to you,' Susanna said flatly. She hated having to do this, she kept her eyes on the window as she spoke, watching the sway of leaves on a lilac bush close to the house. A blue-tit alighted on a branch and then flew off again in a flash of vivid colour. She sighed.

'What about?' Alex asked guardedly, frowning.

The garden was full of sunlight and heady with the scent of flowers, the cottage was quiet and peaceful, the only sound the regular, measured movement of the grandfather clock in the hall; yet Susanna felt instinctively that she had brought with her into this paradise the menacing dark shadow of Niall Ardrey. His threat lay over them almost tangibly as they drew together like nervous children, waiting for her to go on.

'I had a visitor this morning. Niall Ardrey.' She dropped her bombshell hurriedly, wanting to get it over with, her voice husky, and saw Sîan turn white and Alex flush to his hair.

After a moment, Alex said slowly: 'He can't have. He's in the States. New York. He isn't due back for weeks.'

'He came back unexpectedly, it seems.' Susanna looked at Sîan who was as tense as a coiled spring, her skin stretched far too tightly over her fine-boned, haunting little face. She bore no resemblance whatever to her brother except in colouring. She had not inherited Niall Ardrey's height or muscular strength. Her eyes were the deep dark blue of gentians, her lids pale and shadowed, almost transparent, fringed with thick black lashes which at that moment seemed to be faintly wet as though she had cried without anyone hearing her.

'He got your letter yesterday.'

Sîan's lips parted and rounded in an O, but she didn't make a sound.

'He told you all about it?' Alex said, thinking aloud, his face draining of colour.

'Yes. I was all at sea at first, of course. Didn't have a clue what he was talking about. How could I have? I've never heard of Sîan or of Niall Ardrey himself.' She looked directly at Alex, her brown eyes clear and frank. 'Now have I?'

Alex looked uneasy, as well he might. 'I couldn't tell you, I'm sorry, Susanna, some things you just can't talk about.'

'Ian knew,' she said drily.

'Very little! He'd met Sîan at the flat and he knew I was coming down here this weekend but I didn't tell him we planned to get married.' Alex paused, his frown deepening. 'How did Ardrey know about you, though? From Ian?'

She nodded. 'Don't blame Ian—I gather Ardrey choked my name out of him. He isn't a man who has any scruple about using force to get what he wants.'

'You can say that again! He's a cold-blooded

adding machine, all he cares about is money. He doesn't give two pins about Sîan. He had her locked up in a dreary boarding school for years, she spent most of her holidays with her grandmother and rarely sees her brother, yet he still feels he can dictate what she does and where she goes.'

Susanna hesitated, then said gently: 'She *is* very young, Alex.'

'What's age got to do with it? Some people aren't adults when they're fifty. Others are grown up at sixteen.' Alex bristled aggressively, scowling at her. 'You can't draw a line and say everyone under this age is a child. You can't generalise like that about human beings.'

'The law does, Alex.'

'The law's an ass, you know that, and the people who make the laws are asses, too.'

Susanna laughed. 'Maybe, but I doubt if that argument will impress the police.' She looked at Sîan and back at Alex. 'Niall Ardrey says that if Sîan isn't back home tonight, he's going to the police.'

'The police!' Sîan gasped, clutching Alex's arm with both hands. 'Oh, Alex!'

'Don't let him frighten you. What can the police do? You'll be eighteen soon and then you'll be legally of age anyway.'

'Alex,' Susanna said wearily.

'What?' He looked at her with defiance, his brown hair pushed back from his face by one hand while the other held Sîan closely. He looked older, more mature, his face toughened by an angry emotion—yet at the same time he looked pathetically young and anxious and Susanna's heart ached for him as she read the misery behind that defiant stare.

'Even if it's true that the police won't be able to do much, except postpone your marriage until Sîan's legally of age, you're fooling yourself if you think that's all that matters. Is isn't that simple and you know it. Whatever you think of Niall Ardrey—whatever I think of him, come to that— one fact's inescapable. He is Sîan's brother. You can't just ignore him. You can't even blame him for being worried when he hears that his seventeen-year-old sister plans to marry someone who hasn't any money and has obvious difficulty in settling down. Niall Ardrey has done a lot of checking up on you; he knows all about your various jobs and the way you've drifted ever since you left school. If I was in his shoes, I'd be worried myself.'

Alex went red as he listened to her and he was obviously on the point of interrupting several times.

When she did stop talking he broke out fiercely: 'I know I had quite a few jobs but I've settled down now, I enjoy working at the agency, I'm good at it and I'm sure I'm going to be successful in advertising. I just didn't know what I wanted to do in the beginning—now, I do. I don't earn a fortune, but Sîan's going to get a job, and together we'll earn quite enough to live on.'

'What about her place at university?' Susanna asked, taken aback.

'She doesn't want to go to university, she never did—all that was her brother's idea. Sîan's not academic, they made her work like mad at that boarding school and she scraped through her exams, but she was bored stiff the whole time and the idea of spending another three years studying and taking exams is more than she can stand.'

Susanna turned her head to look at Sîan, questioning surprise in her face. Sîan was leaning on Alex now, her slender body still tense.

'Tell her,' Alex said, rubbing his cheek on the girl's sleek hair.

Sîan looked nervously at Susanna. 'It's true, I don't want to go to university, I told Niall but he wouldn't listen. He said I was just being silly. He wants me to have a degree; he thinks a degree is the answer to everything.' She stopped speaking and broke away from Alex to run out of the room. They heard her sobbing as she tore upstairs then a door slammed and Alex scowled at Susanna.

'You've upset her, why did you come?'

'I had to, don't be an idiot, Alex. How do you think I felt when Niall Ardrey came bursting into the flat this morning with that story? I had the devil of a job convincing him that I didn't have Sîan hidden away under my bed. He searched my flat.'

'Searched your flat?' Alex looked furious. 'You shouldn't have let him!'

'I didn't have much of an option—he barged in and set about searching it before I knew what was going on.'

'Who does he think he is?' Alex muttered, beginning to pace the floor like an expectant father, his hands clasped behind his back and his head bent.

'He knows very well who he is; he's Sîan's elder brother and he's a very rich man, I gather.' She eyed her brother reflectively. 'Did you know he owned the firm you work for?'

'Yes,' Alex said vaguely. His hair was several shades darker than Susanna's and had none of the glowing red which made her hair like mahogany in sunlight. His eyes were darker, too. Susanna had eyes of a warm, soft brown but Alex's were deep and very dark, almost black. He had always been restless and over-mobile, even as a small child; he never walked when he could run or sat about in chairs, reading, as Susanna had done. He had been active from morning to night, driving their mother frantic when she could not find him as night fell. His mind was as restless as his body; he was always excited by new horizons and new ideas.

'Didn't it occur to you that he might get your boss to sack you if you married his sister against his will?' Susanna said carefully and Alex turned to face her, startled.

'Did he say he would?'

She nodded.

Alex grimaced. 'Well, I'm not surprised, of course; I had considered the possibility. But I'll get another job. Now I know what I want to do, what I can do, I'm sure I'll be able to get a job in another advertising agency.'

'You're not being practical, Alex. What are the two of you going to live on?'

'We'll have the money I'm supposed to inherit when I marry—that should buy us a flat.' He looked down, very red. 'If the worst came to the worst I thought we could always live here, after all you aren't using it and. . . .'

'You could, of course,' Susanna said calmly. 'I wouldn't stop you, but it would take you hours to drive to London every day and by the time you got back here at night you'd be exhausted.'

'It could be done, though.' Alex sat down at the kitchen table, his shoulders slumping. 'I love her, Susie. I can't bear the idea of saying goodbye to her. She's the first person I've ever felt I could live with for the rest of my life. You don't know her; she's gentle and sensitive and easily hurt and she needs me to look after her. Ardrey doesn't love her, nobody but me loves her. We're happy together, I don't believe I'll ever meet anyone so right again.'

Susanna slowly went over to ruffle his hair lightly, her face unhappy. Alex leaned back to look up at her, pleadingly.

'I'd do anything to keep her with me; I'll work on a farm or get a job digging roads, I don't mind what I do so long as Sîan's with me, and she feels the same way.'

Susanna sighed. 'Well, I don't know about you, but all this emotion is making me very hungry. I'll get the lunch. You go and talk to Sîan and bring her down to eat it in ten minutes.'

Alex got up, nodding, but did not leave the room for a moment. 'Susie, did you tell Ardrey that we might be here?' he asked hesitantly.

She smiled at him. 'No, I didn't feel like telling Mr Ardrey anything.'

Alex hugged her then self-consciously bolted out of the door. Susanna looked after him as he thudded up the stairs, her expression wry. There was a great deal of the adolescent in Alex even now; perhaps losing their mother had been a deeper shock to him than she had thought? Or was it the loss of their father years earlier? It could not be easy for a restless, energetic boy to grow up without a father. Their mother had spoilt him, she had always had a secret preference for her son and Susanna had known it long ago. It had not hurt her, she had been fond enough of both of them to accept the fact without resenting it, but she had noticed it and realised, too, that their mother leaned on Alex, clung to him more than she might have done if she had not lost her husband so tragically early in their marriage.

Had it been that smothering dependence which had made Alex so restless, as he got older? He had loved their mother, Susanna didn't doubt that— but had her clinging made Alex want to get away, all the same? Susanna could remember her mother trying to stop Alex going out on a cold day, or draping him with thick woollen scarves, terrified that he might have inherited his father's weak chest and tendency to catch cold, and Alex had wriggled and protested but always given in because his mother became so agitated if he refused to do as she asked.

Perhaps Alex had been torn between a wish to please his mother and a resentment of her which, when she died, made him feel guilty, self-reproachful. His character had probably been partly inherited from both his parents, but environment played a part in forming character, too, and in some ways Alex had been a deprived child. He had been deprived of a father, deprived of freedom from responsibility because his mother demanded so much from him. If he stayed out late with his friends, playing football or riding on his bicycle, his mother fretted and reproached him. Love could be as claustrophobic as a locked room in some circumstances.

Yet Alex was eager to get married and was picking a girl who was little more than a child, herself, one who would probably lean on him in exactly the way their mother had leant on him.

Susanna sighed, beginning to assemble a salad. People were odd, you could never quite work out why they did what they did, often they didn't seem to have any idea themselves.

She had just finished preparing the lunch when she heard them coming down the stairs. Susanna had a bright smile ready, she was hoping to change their mood if they were as miserable as they had been earlier. One thing was crystal clear—neither of them had thought their plans through and sooner or later they would have to do that.

'Oh, there you are!' she said cheerfully. 'Good, everything's ready—I laid the table in here to save trouble. You don't mind eating in the kitchen, do you, Sîan?'

'Oh, no, of course not.' Sîan sat down opposite Susanna with Alex beside her. It was clear she had been crying, her nose was pink and her lids faintly swollen, but Susanna pretended not to have noticed, passing the oval dish of sliced chicken without a quiver of expression.

Sîan took a small slice and handed the dish to Alex. Susanna helped herself to salad, talking lightly.

'This weather is gorgeous, isn't it? I saw you'd mowed the lawn, Alex—was the grass up to your waist?'

'Pretty well,' he said gruffly, taking the salad bowl from her as she held it out.

'Oh, I hope you like garlic, Sîan. I used it without thinking.'

Sîan nodded without looking up. 'Yes, thank you.'

'We bought it when we got the salad,' Alex pointed out.

'How long have you been down here?' Susanna asked and he shrugged.

'We drove down yesterday.'

There was a little silence. Susanna peered through lowered lashes to observe Sîan's pink face. Alex shifted on his chair, glowering.

'We aren't sharing a room, if that's what's in your mind,' he muttered angrily.

'It wasn't, actually,' Susanna lied softly. There was no point in antagonising him, he was in an excitable and emotional mood already. If she was going to talk them into discussing their plans in a practical way, she had to calm Alex down.

'I ought to have the cottage painted before winter. The woodwork is in a very bad state,' she said and Alex nodded agreement.

For the rest of the meal, Susanna managed to keep the conversation light and general. Sîan didn't say anything much although she answered if Susanna spoke to her; brief, whispered replies which were usually monosyllabic.

'Will you help me with the washing-up, Sîan?' Susanna asked as they finished their coffee some hour later. 'Alex, carry these to the sink, will you?' She pushed their plates into his hands and sulkily he obeyed.

'Any other orders for me?' he asked in that aggressive way, hovering as Susanna began to run water into the plastic bowl.

'No, you can go and sunbathe on the lawn if you like.'

Alex scowled. 'I think I'll go for a walk across the common—I don't feel like sitting about in the sun, it's too hot.'

Susanna laughed. 'Won't it be even hotter, walking?'

But Alex had already gone and the front door banged behind him. Sian picked up the tea-towel which Susanna had pulled out of a drawer a moment earlier.

'He's very upset,' she said defensively.

'I know.' Susanna handed her a plate. 'How long have you known him, Sîan?'

Sîan went pink. 'Oh, nearly two months.' She apparently read Susanna's expression because she said quickly, 'It's long enough to be sure.'

'I've been going out with my own boyfriend for much longer but I wouldn't care to risk marrying him until I know him a lot better.' Susanna wouldn't want to marry Johnny anyway, he wasn't the type of man she had decided she wanted to marry, but she didn't say that.

'Sometimes it happens at once,' Sîan said huskily.

'You've been wiping that plate for nearly five minutes. There won't be any pattern left on it if you go on much longer,' Susanna said teasingly, smiling.

Sîan nearly dropped the plate. 'Oh, sorry!' she said, hurriedly putting it down on the table and picking up another one. It was a few minutes before she spoke again, then she said: 'Was Niall very angry?'

'Very.' Sîan must know what sort of man her brother was! What had she expected? She studied the girl's fragile profile out of the corner of her eye, curious about her.

'Why did you write that letter to him?'

Sîan started, looking at her with a nervous expression. 'Well, I ... I thought I must tell him. ...' She gestured vaguely as though expecting Susanna to finish that sentence and Susanna gave her a wry smile.

'What reaction were you expecting? What were you and Alex planning to do, anyway? Disappear until your eighteenth birthday?'

Sîan seemed shocked, she went pink. 'Oh, no, we only came here for the weekend. Alex has to be back at work tomorrow morning.'

'That's true,' Susanna said, staring at her. 'And what about you? What were you going to do?'

Sîan looked down, biting her lip. 'I ... well, Alex thought I might stay here for a while but we hadn't made up our minds.' She looked up, her huge eyes pleading. 'I didn't realise the cottage was yours. I thought you and Alex owned it between you. I'm sorry.'

'Don't be silly. It's Alex's home as much as mine; he has every right to bring his friends here. Don't even think of it.' Susanna watched the girl uneasily. She looked so young. Had that letter to her brother been an unconscious plea for his attention at last? An attempt to make her brother realise that she wasn't a puppet or a child, she was nearly a woman? From what Alex had said, Niall Ardrey had spent very little time with his sister. He had handed her over to strangers and made no effort to create a home life for her. If Alex had been smothered by too much love, Sîan seemed to have been starved of it altogether.

'Do you like your brother?' Susanna asked as she finished the washing-up and dried her hands.

'Like him?' repeated Sîan, apparently baffled by the question.

Susanna laughed. 'He's an overbearing brute with the manners of Attila the Hun, but he *is* your brother. Do you like him?'

Sîan looked away, as if unwilling to commit herself, then suddenly gave a gasp and dropped the bowl she was drying. It shattered into fragments which flew in all directions. The next second Sîan was running out of the room and up the stairs and in the same instant Susanna heard the front door creak. She had guessed before he appeared in the doorway that it was Niall Ardrey. He had that effect on people.

She looked at him ironically. 'I knew it had to be you when Sîan looked as if she had just seen a cobra.'

He strolled into the kitchen, his black head bent to avoid collision with the top of the door frame, and glanced around the room then back at her.

'I can't say I was flattered by your description of me, but I wasn't meant to be, was I? I'd like to have heard Sîan's answer, though. A pity she saw me first.'

'How did you hear what we were saying?'

He glanced at the kitchen window and she grimaced. 'Oh, I see! You were out there, eavesdropping, were you? I won't give you the usual cliché, and don't expect me to apologise.'

'Oh, I don't,' he said with dislike and they stared at each other coldly.

'How did you get here? Were you following me?'

'My detective was—he rang me once he had this address and I drove down as fast as the road allowed.'

'I knew it,' Susanna said fiercely. 'I knew someone was following me. It was the grey-haired man in a tweed jacket, I wish I'd rammed his car and sent him into a ditch.' She walked over to a cupboard and took out a brush and dustpan.

His brow curved ironically. 'Your family seem fated to make the acquaintance of the police, or do they already have a fat file on you?'

Susanna knelt down to sweep up the fragments of china, ignoring him. A jagged piece of china ran into her thumb and blood oozed from the small wound. She stood up, the brush and dustpan clutched in one hand, sucking the thumb on the other, and Niall Ardrey said sharply: 'Now what have you done to yourself?' She took no notice of him, but briskly emptied the contents of the dustpan into the kitchen waste-bin with a loud clatter, put the brush and pan back into the cupboard and then began washing her hands under the sink tap. She ran cold water on her thumb but the bleeding did not stop.

'Let me see!' Niall Ardrey grabbed her wrist and lifted her hand to stare at her thumb. 'You may have a tiny fragment lodged in there. Have you got a magnifying glass? We may be able to see it.'

'It's nothing,' Susanna said, jerking her hand away, frowning. She resented the peremptory tone, the insistent grip of his long, slim fingers. She dried her thumb carefully, found a sticking plaster in one of the cupboards and deftly bound it over the small cut, aware of him watching her and resenting that, too. He was much too big for the small room, he dominated it by sheer force of size and presence. In any room he would probably be too much, but in such a confined space he was an intolerable pressure on the nerves.

'Where's your brother?'

'Out for a walk. He'll be back soon.' Susanna was anxious as she thought of Alex returning, finding Niall Ardrey here. There was bound to be a confrontation, undoubtedly hostile; Alex would lose his temper and his self-control but this cold-eyed man would do neither. While Alex raged and shouted, Niall Ardrey's grey gaze would strip him of every vestige of self-respect. It is so easy to make a fool of someone whose emotions are involved if you, yourself are totally calm and impregnable. Niall Ardrey had a ruthless face, hard-boned and immovable. Susanna was afraid for her brother. Alex was so sure he could handle the situation and he was so vulnerable, although he wouldn't thank her for saying so.

'Sîan should have had time to quieten down,' he said, glancing at his watch. Susanna saw the crisp cuffs of the shirt beneath his dark grey jacket; the links gleamed, a solid and stylishly simple gold cartouche, with initials engraved on them. That wasn't all she noticed; she saw the fine blue veins where his pulse beat, and a scattering of dark hairs. They made him oddly human, he wasn't built of granite after all, he was flesh and blood, yet that made it worse, didn't it? What sort of human being treats a girl of seventeen the way he was treating his sister? If Sîan's story was the truth, Niall Ardrey thought of her the way he thought of his stocks and shares. He had locked her safely away where nobody could reach her, but he didn't have any feelings for her whatever.

'I'll go up and talk to her now,' he was adding, turning to walk to the door.

Susanna leapt to block his path. 'Leave her alone. She's very upset and. . . .'

'She is my sister, Miss Howard. I came here to talk to her and take her home and that is what I intend to do.' His grey eyes were narrowed and icy.

'This is my house and you were not invited into it,' Susanna said. 'Kindly leave it at once.'

He laughed. For a second she could not believe her ears, she stared at him in furious incredulity, and he gave her a smile which in any other man she would have described as teasingly flirtatious.

'Make me,' he mocked, his long, powerful body at ease yet somehow threatening.

Susanna stared contemptuously at him. 'Oh, yes—*that* you understand, don't you? Threats, force, power—they really make sense to you. In your world it's the strong who count. The weak just get walked over. I asked Sîan if she liked you, she didn't have time to tell me but I don't really need to be told. I shouldn't think anybody likes you, Mr Ardrey. You're not a very likeable man.'

His face had altered; tightened, stiffened, his grey eyes filling with cold anger and his mouth straight and hard.

'Finished?' he asked tersely as she paused, and she laughed angrily.

'No, not yet. Isn't it time you started realising that Sîan is almost a woman? You shut her up in a school for as long as you could, where they would keep her safely out of your way and make sure there was the least possible inconvenience to you. Now you have her back on your hands and you've decided to pack her off to university. You know she doesn't want to go. She told you so, but you brushed that aside, didn't you? Sîan doesn't have a right to an opinion. She isn't a human being to you—she's just one of the family assets and you don't want her to get into the wrong hands. You think that's all she can ever be to anyone else, too. You don't love her you don't believe anyone else ever could either. You're judging my brother by your own standards; you never think of anything else but money so you believe that must be Alex's motive too. You're wrong. Alex loves her.' She paused and he opened his mouth to speak. Susanna spoke first, her voice overriding his because she wasn't going to let him stop her. He thought he could do just as he liked, force his way into her home, interrogate her as though he was a prosecuting counsel, throw his weight around and scare the life out of people, but he wasn't getting away scot-free this time.

'And you needn't sneer—love may be a four-letter word to you but Alex is serious. He's in love and I won't stand by and see him get hurt, especially by someone like you. You're not a human being, you're a computer, a financial think-tank; when you open your mouth to talk, I can practically hear the hum of electricity and the micro-chips cheeping away. . . .'

'Who the hell do you think you're talking to?' he grated and if she had ever thought he was threatening before, she had underestimated his ability to terrify. He took a step and grabbed her shoulders, shaking her violently, so that her rich reddy-brown hair was swirled into a maelstrom. Separate strands of it floated slowly over his hands as he stopped shaking her and held her immobile, like a drooping rag doll, staring up at him in startled shock. It wasn't so much the physical violence, it was the black rage in his face which made her keep still.

His grey eyes glittered like points of icy light. 'You don't know anything about me. Or about Sîan.'

The fingers biting into her flesh hurt. She winced, not daring to take her eyes off him. 'Mr Ardrey, if you don't let go. . . .'

'You talk too damned much,' he said then his gaze moved down over her uplifted face; the brown eyes with their fan of black lashes, the small straight nose and wide, passionate mouth. 'There's only one sure way of keeping a woman quiet,' he said in a new voice.

Susanna's whole body went rigid. 'No,' she said fiercely, but the word was hardly out of her mouth before it was smoothed by the sensual invasion of his lips, forced down abruptly against her own. She struggled helplessly, pulling back her head, and one of his hands slid down her back, pressing her towards him so that she could not escape awareness of his powerful masculinity. She was under no illusions. This was no kiss of passion or desire; it was an angry punishment, a reminder of his male strength. She kept her lips closed against it, hitting him with clenched fists and kicking his calves.

He let go of her and she leaped backwards, trembling. She pulled a clean handkerchief out of the back pocket of her jeans and rubbed it ruthlessly over her mouth then dropped it into the waste bin.

Niall Ardrey watched in silence, then turned on his heel and walked out. She sat down at the kitchen table and tried to control the violent shaking of her body. It was a good ten minutes before she recovered. Rage had done something drastic to her temperature; her body was icy cold one minute, burning with heat the next, and she did not trust her legs. If she tried to stand they might give way under her.

She had not heard a sound from upstairs. Niall Ardrey and Sîan were talking very quietly. She looked at her watch uneasily. Where on earth was Alex? Why didn't he come back?

She felt calm enough by then to make herself some tea. She drank it in the sitting room, standing by the window watching the loop of swallows against the blue sky. Her mother's sewing basket still stood beside the chair she had always sat in; Susanna looked down at it with a sigh. She ought to go through the cottage and sort out her mother's possessions one day. She had never felt up to doing anything about them before; all her clothes had been given away to the church jumble sale last year but so much else remained. They helped to maintain the illusion that this was still a home.

Another glance at her watch told her that Alex had been gone now for well over an hour. He ought to be with Sîan, supporting her against that ruthless swine of a man. Susanna put down her cup and saucer, making up her mind suddenly, and went out of the cottage to see if she could catch sight of Alex on the common, which was only five minutes walk away from the cottage.

There was no sign of him in the lane, but she found him on the far side of the common. He was with an old schoolfriend who still lived in the village. Both men were peering into the engine of a blue car, and when Susanna called Alex did not hear her at first.

She began to run across the grass which was rough and tussocky, colourful with meadow flowers; yellow vetch and toadflax and purple clover busy with bees. The long grass brushed against her jeans and she sneezed as pollen floated up into her nostrils. She yelled again and waved and this time Alex did turn and wave back. A moment later Susanna tripped over a molehill and went down full length. She heard Alex and his friend laughing, but her brother ran over to help her up.

'Hurt yourself? You looked very funny, going flat on your face.' Alex brushed down her jeans where grass stains had smeared them and, breathing rapidly, Susanna pulled herself together.

'Niall Ardrey's at the cottage,' she gasped.

'What?' Alex went pale.

'He had a detective following me!' Susanna went on but she was already talking to herself. Alex had gone without another word. Susanna bent down to rub her knee, wincing. When she fell it had taken most of her weight and it hurt like hell. She must have bruised it badly.

She limped back to the cottage slowly and as she came towards it saw a long, white Jaguar driving away. Susanna could not see the occupants, but she had no difficulty in guessing that the driver was Niall Ardrey.

Alex stood by the gate. As she hobbled towards him he looked round, his face ashen.

'She's gone,' he said in a flat, blank voice. 'She went with him.'

He looked ill; his dark eyes almost sunken in that white face. Susanna put an arm round him, trying to hide her own anxiety.

'Didn't she say anything? What's going to happen now?'

'Say anything? Yes, she said something. She said she was sorry, it wouldn't work. It had been a mistake, she realised now that she was too young to talk about getting married.' He began to laugh but there was no genuine amusement in the laughter, it was painful, and Susanna winced as she listened to it.

'Then she said she hoped she hadn't hurt me but one day I'd realise she was right.' Alex's voice was beginning to be angry, it shook.

Susanna did not say anything, her face as expressionless as she could make it. Niall Ardrey had won, then. What had he said to his sister to make her change her mind? But what did that matter? The only thing that counted was that he had persuaded Sîan to leave Alex and now Susanna had to think of some way of comforting her brother. She put an arm round him, searching for the right words, but Alex pushed her away and stumbled towards his own car, got into it and slammed the door. A second later the engine started and the car took off with a screech of tyres, the wheels sending up a shower of white dust from the road.

Susanna stared after it anxiously. What was Alex going to do now?

CHAPTER THREE

SUSANNA drove back to London an hour later, having spent the intervening time in tidying the cottage. She had hung on, hoping that Alex would return, but as he didn't show up she decided that he must have gone to London. She would ring him as soon as she reached her flat. Alex was in an unpredictable mood; he might do something crazy and Susanna felt an urgent need to talk to him and find out what he meant to do now. Was he going to go on working at the agency? Had Niall Ardrey said anything about that to him? She could not help remembering Niall Ardrey's threat to have Alex fired. He was quite capable of going through with it, too.

Her face glowed with angry colour as she remembered something else—that kiss. It had made her so angry that she had had to keep an icy control on herself, or she might have hit him with the nearest blunt object. It had probably been the single least enjoyable experience in her life. His mouth had been so hard and angry, forcing her lips back on her teeth. It was typical of a guy like that to use sex as a weapon against a woman. If he had been quarrelling with another man, would he have tried to shut him up by kissing him?

She laughed furiously, scaring the life out of another motorist drawn up beside her at a set of traffic lights. He shot one look at her bared teeth

and flashing eyes and almost jumped the lights in
his haste to get away from her.

Susanna was barely aware of him. She drove on
in his wake, worrying about Alex. He would get
over this, of course, but he was not going to
believe that at the moment. She had no doubts
about his sincerity; he was convinced he needed
Sîan and he was clinging to her with all the
obsessive insistence with which his mother had
clung to him. Perhaps he had inherited that trait
from their mother? Or maybe their mother's
behaviour had left an indelible impression on him,
so that the only sort of love he understood and
could feel was the love which clings and smothers?

Why on earth had he picked a girl like Sîan
Ardrey, though? Susanna suspected that Sîan's
emotions were just as tangled. Why else had she
written to her brother before she went off with
Alex? She had wanted to shock Niall Ardrey into
giving her his undivided attention for once—and
she had certainly succeeded. Susanna even
wondered if Sîan had ever felt that much for Alex,
anyway. She did not doubt her brother's feelings,
but Sîan's were less certain.

Alex should have fallen in love with a nice,
down-to-earth girl who would give him the
emotional security he was really looking for.

Susanna smiled wryly to herself at the thought.
Easy to say something like that; but human beings
are never so cool-headed and practical in their love
affairs. All the same, Sian had problems of her
own which Alex was in no way capable of solving.
He could not even work out his own hang-ups;
Susanna suspected he was not even aware of them.
He was too muddled at the moment to see himself

clearly. Some people never see themselves clearly; they live in a world of illusion and makebelieve, especially when they are young.

It was gone six when she drove into the underground car park. She felt very tired; partly because of the strain the events of the day had imposed on her and partly because she had driven so far.

When she got to her flat, she flung off her jacket, kicked off her shoes and went into the kitchen to put on the kettle. She needed a cup of tea; her mouth was parched. While the kettle was humming busily, she went into the bathroom. She hadn't stopped on the road and she was dying to go to the lavatory.

She heard the kettle begin to whistle as she was washing her hands and face; she felt so grubby and hot after the long drive in the afternoon heat. It was pure bliss to let the water run coolly over her skin. Rapidly drying herself, she went back into the kitchen, made the tea and poured herself a cup. Susanna loved China tea, she half-closed her eyes, pleasurably inhaling the delicately scented odour before she added a touch of milk.

Before she drank her tea, however, she had to ring Alex. It wasn't him who answered the phone, though; it was Ian, sounding half asleep.

'Hmm?'

'Ian? Is Alex there? This is Susanna.'

'Oh, hi! No, he isn't. Why did you want him? Is it urgent? I mean, I could. . . .'

'I must talk to him—when he does come in, will you ask him to ring me at once?'

'Well,' Ian said slowly, sounding very guarded. 'I think I may know where he is. . . .'

Susanna smiled wryly. 'I've been down to the cottage, I saw him there.'

'Oh, you did?' Ian's voice altered.

'I wasn't the only visitor, unfortunately.' She heard Ian draw a breath in wary reaction. 'Niall Ardrey had me followed,' she added.

'That man! Nasty piece of work, he practically throttled me.' Ian was a cheerful, even-tempered young man normally; it wasn't like him to snarl but he was definitely snarling now. 'I'm afraid that's my fault. He wouldn't leave without some sort of answer so I told him your name. I thought you were going out today, that he wouldn't find you at home. I'm terribly sorry, Susanna. What happened at the cottage?'

Susanna hesitated. She did not like discussing her brother's private life behind his back, but if Ian did not know what had happened he might put his foot in it, so reluctantly she gave him a brief outline of the day's events and Ian whistled softly.

'Too bad, poor old Alex. Took it badly, did he?'

'Very. I was worried about him. He drove off like a maniac, and I've no idea where he went.'

'He's totally hooked on her, you know. Could never see why, myself—I mean, she's okay, pretty enough in a way, but not my type. I like girls with a bit more flesh. . . .' He broke off, coughing, and hurriedly said: 'Well, I'll tell him when he shows up.'

Smiling, Susanna rang off and sank back on the couch to drink her tea. Five minutes later the phone rang and she jumped up to answer it.

'Alex?'

'No, honey, it's me,' a voice said, and she smiled, relaxing.

'Oh, hallo, Johnny.'

'I've been trying to get you for an hour. Did you settle the family business you went to see Alex about?'

Susanna considered the question with a wry expression in her eyes. 'I think it got settled one way or another,' she conceded after a pause.

'You don't sound too cheerful about it.'

'I'm not but never mind. Why did you ring?'

'To ask you out to dinner. Now, don't say you can't come—I've spent the day lolling about in chairs reading every Sunday newspaper under the sun and I'm bored to the back teeth. Take pity on me.'

'I can't go out, Johnny—I'm waiting for Alex to ring me.'

There was a silence, then Johnny said with a sober accent: 'Honey, are you gently giving me the push?'

'Idiot! Of course not!'

'Then why don't I come round and stop off at a Chinese take-away to get some sweet and sour prawn and duck in lemon sauce?'

'Don't tempt me! I'm hungry and I'd love some Chinese food, but I really am worried about Alex, Johnny. I wouldn't be very good company tonight.'

Johnny was quiet for a moment, then said: 'Do you want company or would you really rather be alone?'

She hesitated before answering. 'I think I'd better take a rain check tonight, Johnny, thanks all the same.'

'Okay, honey, you know where I am if you do want me.' He rang off and she stood at the window, watching the twilight drifting down to cloak London in a lavender mist, turning the silhouettes of church spires and gables into ghostly images. The sun had almost vanished; she just saw the blood-red fringe of it behind a roof. There was something ominous in the reflection of that dying sun on the blue-black slate, and she shivered, staring at it.

'Poor Alex,' she murmured aloud. How must he be feeling? Where was he? She turned away from the window, shaking off her mood and went into her bedroom. She must change out of these grass-stained, dishevelled jeans.

She put on a lemon coloured shirt and a finely pleated cream and tan skirt belted neatly at the waist, brushed her hair, which sent a little shower of grass seed floating into the atmosphere, and lightly glossed her lips with a pink lipstick.

She looked calm and casual. She wished she felt it. Should she make herself a meal? She didn't feel like making the effort, although she was hungry. Looking at her watch she saw it was now gone seven.

She wandered over to her desk beside the window in the sitting room and sat down to look at the work she was currently doing; a series of illustrations for a children's book of fairy tales. The text had something eerie about it and Susanna was trying to reproduce that feel in her illustrations; pointed-eared goblins with malicious faces peered from behind bushes, tree trunks were half human, the knots in the bark turning into eyes and the branches grasping with twiggy fingers, as children ran by. Each picture was crowded with such detail, often minute and delicately done. She was enjoying the work, it was quite different to the last job she had had, a very down-to-earth set of illustrations for a book set on a Welsh farm. She had visited Wales for a fortnight to get the background for that, which had been the most enjoyable part of the job. The worst part had been painting a black and white cow. It had taken her days and been very concentrated; she had had to be exact, every muscle and detail perfect, but the cow had not been a very good sitter. She had moaned plaintively, shifted her feet, swished her tail, tossed her head and kept trying to escape.

Susanna preferred the work she was doing now; it gave her an unusual opportunity to use her own imagination, unfettered by the demands of the text, since she merely had to make sure that the pictures reflected the stories and were timeless in their appearance.

When the door bell rang she jumped, startled, then leapt up and almost ran to the front door. It had to be Alex. It must be Alex. She fumbled with the handle and felt one of her nails break but at least the door was wrenched open and she gave a deep sigh of relief when she saw her brother.

'Alex, where have you been? I've been so worried about you, why did you shoot off like that?' she burst out and then could have kicked herself because she had not meant to scold him, he had enough problems without her letting off steam.

'I had to get away on my own,' he said sullenly, walking down the corridor. 'I just drove around and thought things out.' His shoulders were slumped and his face still pale but she saw that anger had replaced the pain which had been in his eyes, and in a way that was a good sign. Alex had reason to be angry. Sîan may have been wise to go back to her home, but she had not really softened the blow for Alex. She might have been more gentle when she told him her decision; it had been a body blow which almost knocked Alex over.

'Have you eaten? Can I get you some food? I haven't eaten myself yet, I was just thinking about cooking a meal.'

'I'm not hungry,' he said, then added brusquely, 'Thanks.' He put a hand into his jacket pocket and brought out something that gleamed. 'I just found this in the car—it's Sîan's, she must have dropped it without noticing. Will you take it back to her?'

Susanna took it as he held it out to her, staring down at it. It was a slim gold compact, square and elegantly designed, with the initials SA picked out on the lid in sapphires.

Susanna whistled softly. 'It looks very expensive.'

'It is valuable, far too valuable to put in the post. It must be taken back by hand. I couldn't bear to see her again.' Alex looked at her pleasingly. 'Will you do it, Susie?'

Reluctantly, she nodded. 'I'll take it back tomorrow—you'd better give me her address.'

'Not tomorrow, it must go back tonight, I don't want it sitting around. What would happen if it was stolen or got lost? I feel uneasy about having it. That swine Ardrey might call in the police, say I'd stolen it—he's capable of it.'

Susanna could not deny that, Niall Ardrey was capable of anything and would have no compunction about accusing Alex of stealing. She sighed, nodding. 'Okay, I'll do it tonight—what's her address?'

'She probably won't have gone back to the people she was staying with—she must be at her brother's house.' Alex handed her a scrap of paper with an address scribbled on it in uneven letters. 'I looked it up in a phone box. He isn't often there, he's one of these jet-setting types who are abroad all the time, but unless he took Sîan to her grandmother in the country, that's where she must be.'

'I'll get my jacket.' Susanna went into her bedroom and came back a moment later to find Alex standing exactly where she had left him; his face sombre and his body tense. He seemed to be in a state of dull shock now. What he needed was food and a couple of glasses of whisky, she thought anxiously. He had to sleep tonight.

'Wait here, won't you?' she begged. 'When I get back I'll cook a meal and we'll talk. Don't go wandering off again, Alex. You're not well.'

'I'm okay,' he said obstinately. 'Make sure you give the compact to Sîan herself.'

'But you'll wait here?'

Shrugging he said: 'If you like.' Susanna relaxed a little more.

'Any message for Sîan?'

He looked at her angrily. 'No!'

She wished she had not asked, but only nodded and went out closing the door quietly behind her. What can you do for someone who is hurt and unhappy except feed them, soothe them into forgetting for a little while? If Alex had broken a leg or had the flu, she wouldn't have any doubts about what to do, but emotional pain is not as easy to deal with and Alex would not want her to probe and question and be open about her concern. He had talked in a curt, harsh way which was totally foreign to his nature. He was pushing away her sympathy, refusing to let her too close, and she had no option but to accept that.

As she drove towards the part of Mayfair where Niall Ardrey lived she wondered if Alex had really been in love with Sîan, or whether his infatuation had been partly illusory? Ian had said he could not understand what Alex saw in her, but then Ian was a pretty well-integrated man with few hang-ups and his interest in the opposite sex was very down-to-earth, not to say earthy. Alex was not as uncomplicated. Sîan was an appealing girl and if Alex had been telling the truth their relationship had not been sexual, they had not got to that stage. They had probably been drawn to each other because they sensed that they had much in common. They were both unhappy, for different reasons, and a mutual unhappiness can turn into sympathy and rapidly from that into a form of love, which is almost self-love and is not very real.

Her mouth tightened and she grimaced as she turned into the road where Niall Ardrey lived. She might have guessed it would look like this—well-preserved Regency houses faced with white stucco and elegant porticoes with slim pillars supporting the roofs above the front doors. Susanna could imagine how much such a house would cost, both to buy and in annual upkeep. Slowing down she began to watch the numbers painted on the columns.

She stopped the car outside the house she was looking for a few seconds later, but did not get out. She leaned on the steeing wheel; staring at the blank, bland façade with a strong feeling of antagonism. It was no doubt thought very beautiful, she had heard people raving about houses like these, had even drawn some of them when she illustrated a hardback edition of Jane Austen a year earlier. Her eye could not help revelling in the perfect proportions of windows and door and in any other circumstances she would have been excited by the chance to see the interior but she refused to be impressed by anything Niall Ardrey owned.

She was not looking forward to meeting either him or Sîan again, but it had to be done so she nerved herself to get out of the car and walk purposefully up the steps, to ring the bell.

After a moment the door opened and a slim woman with iron-grey hair, wearing a dove-grey dress, looked at her questioningly. 'Yes?'

'I would like to see Miss Ardrey, please,' Susanna said in a stiff voice.

'Miss Ardrey?' The woman frowned, half glancing behind her, and Susanna's gaze moved in the same direction, along the spacious high-ceilinged hall. The floor was tiled in white stone but deep Turkish carpets covered most of it and the walls were painted a smooth aqueous blue, with white and gold panels at intervals. Although her eye took in these background details, it was at the man standing at the far end of the hall that Susanna stared, stiffening further.

'All right, Mrs West,' Niall Ardrey said, strolling forward and the woman nodded, turning away. Susanna stood on the threshold, her hands in her jacket pockets because her fingers were

suddenly icy cold. Niall Ardrey had that effect on
her every time she saw him, he made her violently
angry and intensely nervous at the same time.

'Come in,' he said tersely and she shook her
head.

'I brought this back for Sîan—she left it in my
brother's car, he only just found it.' She pulled a
hand out of her pocket and offered him the
compact.

He held it, turning it in his fingers while she
watched. His hands were more elegant and
graceful than they had any right to be; it annoyed
her to have to admire their supple, smooth
movements. His nails were probably professionally
manicured, she thought with a faint grimace. They
were perfectly shaped and regular.

'You can't see Sîan, she has gone to bed,' he
said, looking up.

'Locked her in her room, did you?'

'Don't be childish, Miss Howard,' he said drily.

Susanna was so angry at that that she broke
out: 'Are you going to have my brother fired?'

His face tightened, the bones under his brown
skin prominent and his jawline fierce. 'I'm not
discussing my private affairs on my doorstep.
Come in!' His hand shot out and grabbed her,
yanked her into the house. Susanna broke free but
by then the front door had been slammed shut, the
sound echoing in the vast hall.

'Will you stop manhandling me?' she said
furiously. 'I won't be pushed around, I'm not one
of your family. I know you get your own way with
them, but I'm a different proposition.'

He looked at her oddly, his brows a sardonic arc
and his eyes coldly penetrating. 'You are indeed.'

He stood back, gesturing with one hand. 'Will you come into my study, Miss Howard? We can talk more privately there.' His tone was mockingly formal.

Susanna was about to refuse when her eye was drawn to a faint movement at the top of the stairs. She caught a brief glimpse of Sîan in a long white nightdress, looking like a ghost, her face as white as the material of the nightdress, then Sîan ducked out of sight again. Susanna reconsidered and walked down the hall with Niall Ardrey on her heels like a sheepdog trailing a recalcitrant charge.

Sîan had looked far from happy. How had her brother persuaded her to go back with him? Had he used threats or persuasion?

'Can I offer you a drink?' he asked, closing the study door behind him.

'I'd like some coffee,' Susanna said and he lifted his brows again.

'I've got some very good brandy.'

'I don't drink spirits, thank you.'

'I'll ask Mrs West to make some coffee,' he said on a resigned note and went out. Susanna stood in the doorway, looking up the stairs. Niall Ardrey had gone through a baize door, she saw it swing softly shut behind him, and the next minute Sîan was leaning over the bannisters. She looked alarmed as she saw Susanna and was about to duck out of sight again when Susanna stepped forward and said quietly: 'Hallo, Sîan. Are you okay?'

Sîan's eyes darted around the hall in a hunted way. Susanna said: 'Your brother has gone to find Mrs West, it's okay.'

Sîan gave a sigh. 'Is Alex very angry?' she whispered.

'He's upset. What do you expect?'

'Tell him . . . oh, I don't know what to tell him. I had to go, there was no point in dragging it out, it would have been more than I could bear. I didn't want to. . . .'

Susanna watched her, frowning. 'Then why did you go?'

'Niall's right, you see. I'd have ruined Alex's life.'

'Nonsense! Is that what he told you?'

'But he is right—I am too young, I suppose I knew that all along. I shouldn't have let it go so far, I was so miserable and Alex was wonderful, but it was just a sort of dream, I never really believed it in. I mean, being married. Talking about it was one thing, but I am too young and if I had married Alex I'd have made him unhappy. I do love him, but I'm not really ready to be married—I hadn't thought about afterwards, you see. I just thought of Alex asking me, it was so flattering, nobody ever wanted me before and. . . .' She broke off as the baize door swung open. Sîan gave Susanna a silent, pleasing look and vanished.

Niall Ardrey halted mid-stride and stared at Susanna, then looked upwards, over his shoulder. There was nothing for him to see, of course, but he turned to give Susanna a dry smile, as if he guessed that she had been talking to Sîan.

Susanna walked back into the study and sat down on a black leather chair. Deep and comfortable, it faced a large portrait in oils which hung over the fireplace. Susanna studied that intently, pretending to be unaware of the man who had followed her into the room.

'My grandmother,' he said a few feet away.

'She was very beautiful; she reminds me of Sîan.' The girl in the picture had the same haunting bone structure and deep, mournful blue eyes but she had something else, a sweet, gentle smile which held a hint of mischief and a rounded, stubborn chin with more than a hint of determination. It was a much happier, much stronger face than Sîan's, although the family resemblance was blazingly obvious.

Mrs West came into the room carrying a large tray on which stood a silver coffee pot and matching cream jug and sugar bowl, and two cups and saucers. She laid it on a low table and looked at Niall Ardrey. 'Shall I pour it for you, sir?'

'Please, Mrs West.'

The woman gave Susanna a polite smile. 'Black or white, Miss?'

'Black, please, no sugar.'

She was given a cup a second later, then Mrs West gave Niall Ardrey his cup. She had not asked him whether he wanted black or white, of course, Susanna noted. She was obviously the housekeeper. How often did he stay in London? Alex had said he was always abroad, but she saw a clutter of papers on the desk against which he was leaning and the room had a lived-in atmosphere suggesting that it was in constant use. The carpet was old and faintly worn in places, the red velvet curtains looked as if they had been in position for years. It was a comfortable, book-lined, cluttered room which was mellow in the lamplight. Lamps stood here and there, on tables and the desk, but not all of them were in use. Niall Ardrey obviously preferred a soft light, no doubt it made it easier to work.

The study was spacious and high-ceilinged, but Niall Ardrey still managed to dominate and dwarf it. She resisted the temptation of looking at him as he drank his coffee, she kept her eyes elsewhere, assessing the objects surrounding him, as though they might give her a clue to the man who owned them.

He put down his cup. 'Your brother needn't worry about his job,' he said coolly. 'I was angry when I made that threat.'

'And now that you've won, you can afford to be magnanimous?' Susanna said with a barbed contempt which made his eyes glitter.

'You have the usual female problem, Miss Howard. You don't know when to hold your tongue.'

'And that's another form of threat, isn't it? Or blackmail might be the better description. What you're implying is that if I'm not careful how I talk to you, my brother will suffer. You think you hold all the cards. Alex needs his job and you can make sure he loses it. Does it give you a big thrill to have that sort of power? I suppose it does. Power's a sex substitute, it can. . . .'

He bent towards her, snarling. 'Don't you ever stop talking? Sex substitute? Do you really think I need one?' Close to he was even more overpowering, as she had already realised; his powerful body had poised vitality, a leashed menace which was intensely sexy although every nerve in Susanna's body quivered in angry protest at her own awareness of that. Sexual magnetism is impossible to define; it can take too many forms. Niall Ardrey's strong face and cold grey eyes, the sardonic assurance of his voice, the hardness of his mouth and the force of his jawline combined to make him a potentially explosive lover but Susanna refused to react to that male strength with anything but rejection. She wasn't going to let herself be vulnerable to a man like Niall Ardrey; she cherished her independence too much. Whatever else he might offer, he wouldn't offer freedom, he had the instincts of the tyrant, and Susanna had no intention of becoming a slave, to him or any other man.

She held on to her temper with a struggle and handed him her cup. 'I'm not interested in your sex life, Mr Ardrey, and now that you've reassured me about my brother I must go.'

He put her cup on the desk, shifting as she rose; not to let her pass but to block her way.

'I'm interested in *your* sex life,' he said mockingly. 'Is there one? What sort of men do you fancy, Miss Howard? Men that you can manipulate? The sort that let you dictate terms and meekly do as you tell them?'

'You seem to see love affairs as battles, maybe yours are—mine aren't.' Susanna turned sideways to escape and he moved again to stop her, his eyes gleaming with an amusement she did not share.

'Have there been many? Love affairs, I mean.'

'Do you want the whole list?' Susanna gave him a tight smile and had a shock when she found herself looking straight into his eyes. They were silvery now, the black centres hypnotic, seeming fathomless as she stared into them. Her mouth was suddenly dry and it didn't make her feel any easier when Niall Ardrey smiled slowly.

'Is it a long one?'

She shrugged and didn't answer that. 'This is a

very stupid discussion; pointless! I must go, I only wanted to bring Sîan's compact back. My brother was afraid you'd accuse him of having stolen it if it wasn't taken back the minute he found it.'

He frowned then, becoming angry again. 'I see. That was your only reason for coming?'

Astonished, she said: 'Of course—what did you think . . .' then broke off, flushing. 'What *did* you think?' That she had leapt at a chance to come here and see him again? He smiled mockingly and her flush deepened. So he thought that, did he? She had met conceited men often enough before, but he was in a class of his own if he really thought she would grab at any excuse to see him after what he had done to her brother. She was shaking with temper as she almost yelled at him.

'Don't kid yourself! I wouldn't cross a road to see you again. In fact, I'd cross a three-lane highway just to avoid you. If you weren't so sold on yourself it would have dawned on you by now that I am not one of your admirers.'

'You have a hot temper,' he observed, almost as though noting the fact for future reference.

'You'd better believe it,' she assured him almost in a hiss.

'And a great deal too much to say for yourself,' he added.

'Oh, nuts,' Susanna muttered, scowling.

'And you're not even pretty,' he informed her, seeming amused when her flush became hectic and her eyes deadly.

'Thank you. Anything else, before I leave? You might as well say it all.'

'But,' he said and paused for a second, surveying her thoughtfully. 'But, there's something about you. Your eyes are amazingly eloquent; even when you aren't talking I can read what you're thinking in your eyes.'

Susanna focused an angry stare on him. 'Like now, for instance?'

His hard mouth curved in amusement. 'Like now,' he agreed with bland mockery. 'Oh, yes, they talk very audibly. And apart from your eyes, there's your mouth, of course.'

That was when Susanna began to get really nervous; she didn't like the way he was staring intently at her mouth. It reminded her too vividly of the way he had kissed her in the cottage, and she felt a tremor of angry excitement against which she struggled furiously. He used sexuality as a weapon; she knew that and she would be insane if she forgot it now.

He moved closer, she could feel his body warmth only inches from her own, and that accelerated the rate of her pulse. 'You have more energy than any woman I've ever met, too,' he said without taking his gaze from her mouth. 'It's like a fire inside you. I'm sure most men sense it the minute they see you. Do you know what that tells them? That you'd be red-hot in bed.' His mouth was posed just above hers, but Susanna moved first. Her slap almost knocked him back across the room and she did not wait for him to recover his balance, she ran towards the door, trembling from head to foot with a burning rage which had not been satisfied by that one hefty slap.

She had opened the door and was running down the hall before he came after her. She did not have to look round to know that he was now as angry as she was; she could sense it in his uneven breathing. She fumbled with the front door, cursing under her breath. Niall was there a second later, his hands descending on her arms like iron clamps, making her wince.

'You little bitch. . . .'

He dragged her towards him, struggling, then the front door bell rang noisily just above them and they both jerked out of their intent involvement with each other, eyes startled. Niall let go of her and she took a shaky step backward.

The next moment Mrs West was walking softly down the hall. Susanna could not look at her, she was too flushed and shaken.

'I'll deal with it, Mrs West,' Niall said in a deep, unsteady voice. He opened the front door, and Susanna saw him dragging a polite smile into his flushed face. The little group of people under the portico moved forward, beaming.

'Hello, Oliver; Esmé, you look marvellous, what a beautiful suit. Jill, you're a knock-out. Come in, all of you. Mrs West will fix you drinks.'

'Such a lovely evening, Niall, I hardly needed my wrap,' said the older of the two women. Middle-aged, with well-styled silvery grey hair, she was wearing evening dress of a fairly daring kind for her age; a tight-fitting wild silk top cut very low and a pair of matching culottes. The salmon-pink shade of the silk was startling. The outfit did not suit her; her figure was too mature and her neck too lined to be flattered by it.

The man with her was pink-faced and immaculate in conservative black evening dress. He stood about with his hands behind his back, looking uncomfortable. The thinning line of his grey hair gave him a noble brow but his features reflected nothing but good-humoured uncertainty about himself and why he was there. His eyes fell on Susanna who was waiting for a chance to get out of the house once they were all inside it. He smiled, nodded. Susanna managed a faint smile back.

'How's Sîan?' the third of the newcomers asked Niall. 'Is she feeling better this evening? Poor sweet, summer colds are the worst, aren't they, Daddy? Whenever I get one I'm in bed for days.'

'Oh, yes, absolutely,' her father mumbled, pleased to be able to agree with someone about something. 'Summer colds, terrible things.'

'Jill, darling, give Mrs West your wrap,' the older woman reminded and the girl gave a brilliant smile to Niall, turning her back to him.

'Would you, Niall?'

He deftly slid the white fur down from her arms and shoulders and while he was otherwise occupied Susanna shot through the door and down the steps. She was at her car a few seconds later. She found the key, unlocked the door and got behind the wheel. The engine started first time and she moved out from the kerb just as Niall Ardrey came into view on the portico of his house. Susanna ignored him and drove away.

CHAPTER FOUR

'WHAT on earth's the matter with Alex these days?' Johnny asked, settling into his seat and opening his programme. The theatre was almost full and the curtain about to go up any minute, they had been late arriving because Johnny had not been able to find anywhere to park and had circled around the West End for nearly half an hour before he managed to inch his small car into a space which Susanna had not thought looked large enough to hold a bicycle. Johnny looked up, when she did not answer, and gave her a questioning look. 'He's very down, isn't he? When I saw him at your flat the other day he barely said a word to me. Have I done something to offend him—or is he as depressed as he seemed?'

'He's very depressed,' Susanna admitted ruefully. It was two weeks since Alex took Sîan down to the cottage, and had his dreams blown to smithereens by Niall Ardrey. Alex was back at work and Susanna had not seen much of him during these two weeks but when she did see him he rarely had much to say. Susanna had had a brief chat with Ian about it one evening when she dropped in at their flat and Ian had told her that he was trying to get Alex out of his withdrawn, silent mood by inviting people round to the flat for supper or dragging Alex, against his will, to an occasional party. It did not seem to be making any impact; Alex was shut up inside himself and refused to talk

about Sîan or respond to Ian's well-meant
attempts to cheer him up.

'Serious?' Johnny asked with a real concern that
Susanna responded to with a warm smile.

'A love affair that didn't work out,' she said
vaguely and Johnny whistled and nodded.

'I know the feeling. Well, at least he'll get over
that. It's bad while it lasts but he'll come out of it
sooner or later.'

Susanna laughed, giving him a wry look. 'I
didn't think you took love that seriously, Johnny.'

'Not any more,' he agreed with a wicked grin.
'A burnt child fears the fire, and all the other
clichés. It was years ago, anyway. I was younger
than Alex and she was older than Eve and twice as
lethal. She handed me the apple, I ate it and was
very sick for a long time. After that, I gave up
intense love affairs.'

She watched him, wondering what exactly lay
behind the casual, mocking words. 'Phrase-maker!
If I didn't know you were a writer, I'd be able to
guess from the way you talk.'

He turned his bright blue eyes on her, amused and
interested. 'Would you? How astute of you. But
you're wrong, you know; we come in all shapes and
sizes, just like anybody else. Most of the writers I
know barely open their mouths in public; they save
all their eloquence for the printed page.'

The lights began to dim, people shuffled and
coughed in anticipation and Johnny settled his
long legs with a sigh of pleasure. 'My favourite
moment,' he whispered. 'I get the same thrill every
time the curtain goes up, especially when I'm going
to see something by Shaw. He never fails to grab
you with that spectral hand.'

The curtain had swished slowly up and someone behind them made a loud shushing noise. Johnny pulled a horrible face and Susanna stifled a laugh as she turned her attention to the stage.

The revival of *Major Barbara* was engrossing. Susanna forgot where she was and who was sitting beside her, so that when the lights went up for the interval she was almost surprised to see Johnny, who grinned at her in comprehending amusement.

'Good, isn't it? I saw you leaning forward, totally hooked.'

She laughed. 'It's marvellous. I'd forgotten how absorbing it is—I haven't seen it for years. It isn't one of those plays which are always being revived, like *Pygmalion* or *Man and Superman*. I suppose it is more dated than they are. We don't have the same problem today.'

Johnny's brows rose. 'Don't we? No alcoholism, Susanna? Are you kidding?'

'We don't try to solve it with religion,' she said drily. 'And before you say so, we're just as confused about arms manufacture too, but we certainly wouldn't fall for all the paternalistic stuff about how the manufacturers give their workers a better life. Whenever I see a Shaw play I'm impressed and amused but never convinced by his arguments; he's a conjuror not a philosopher.'

'But what a showman,' Johnny said with excited admiration. His hand pushed back the lock of ash-blond hair which always seemed to be falling over his forehead. His hair was very fine and soft, Susanna had often envied him that colour. 'All the same, I think he was on the right track—what he was really saying was that if people had a better life they wouldn't need to fall back on drink.'

'I've known some very rich alcoholics,' Susanna said, and Johnny made a face.

'True, so have I. Talking of which, shall we make for the bar? It's very warm in here and I'm thirsty.'

Most of their row had already headed towards the bar. They edged their way along the seats into the aisle. 'Full house, I'd say,' Johnny murmured, glancing around, and Susanna's gaze followed his without real interest.

The bar was packed; they had to force their way through groups of loudly exclaiming people. Susanna squeezed herself between two men, muttering: 'Excuse me,' and got an irritated look from each of them as they addressed each other over her head.

'The shares rocketed next day, absolutely rocketed.'

'Well, there you are, then—never can tell, funny animal, the market.'

Johnny looked back at her, his hand reaching for hers. 'Hang on to me, honey, or you'll lose me in this crush.'

'We'll never get a drink before the bell goes,' she said gloomily and Johnny grinned at her.

'I ordered them before we went in, they're waiting for us on the shelf over there, unless some swine has made off with them. I ordered you a lemonade and ice—okay?'

'You're wonderful,' Susanna said with fervour and he laughed, tugging her through a tiny gap between two groups. One of the left-hand group turned to look at her and with a shock of recognition she stared into Niall Ardrey's face.

He seemed as taken aback as Susanna; his grey eyes narrowed and his brows lifted in a silent comment. She should have recognised him even from the back; his height, the aggressive width of his shoulders and that thick, vital black hair were unmistakable.

She did not have time to decide whether or not to admit she knew him. Before either of them could say anything Johnny was pulling her away. She was flushed when she reached the corner of the bar and had a glass put into her hand; but Johnny assumed that the struggle to reach their drinks had caused the pinkness of her cheeks and her slight breathlessness.

'Mmm ... I needed this,' he said, swallowing some of his own drink, a pint of lager. 'My mouth is as dry as a kiln. Drink up, Susanna. The bell will be going soon.'

Susanna gulped down some of her lemonade; it was deliciously refreshing although the ice had already begun to melt in the heat of the room. My heart is beating very fast, she thought almost anxiously. What on earth is the matter with me? She could feel the pulses throbbing at her wrists and the base of her throat and she was very hot. How odd, she told herself. Anger has a remarkably disturbing effect on the metabolism. She had never noticed before how much it affected her. When she saw Niall Ardrey just now, though, she had felt her whole body jerk with a sort of shock; her blood had begun to run faster in her veins, her face had heated and the hair at the back of her neck had bristled the way a cat's fur bristles when it sees a dog. It must be a surge of adrenalin, I suppose, she thought; anger and fear are closely allied and Niall Ardrey has been a threat to me ever since he forced his way into my flat.

Johnny was talking lightly about the play. She half-listened, half-struggled to calm herself. It was ridiculous to let someone like Niall Ardrey upset her; it could ruin her evening. She had been enjoying herself until she saw him.

'You're very quiet,' Johnny said, frowning. He had a firmly fleshed face, and his features were regular, well-proportioned, distinctly pleasing to the eye without being precisely handsome. The smile he normally wore was his chief attraction; it was light-hearted and friendly and immediately made people like him.

'Sorry,' she said, smiling at him. 'It's so hot in here, I suppose. All this noise makes it difficult to concentrate. I hate crowds; there's something scary about them. Even when they're good-humoured you never know what they might do if they got out of control.'

'I saw a crowd run mad once in India,' Johnny said, plunging into a long anecdote to which she listened in dismay, finishing her drink. The bell went just as she put down her glass and the crowded bar began to empty slowly.

As they made their way back to their seats, Johnny said quietly: 'I get the feeling you're still worried about Alex. You spend too much time trying to straighten his life out for him, Susanna. He's a big boy now. Let him have a shot at getting himself together without your help for once. It wouldn't do him any harm. Ever since I've known you, you've been lending him money, cooking and cleaning for him, generally playing the mother hen. While you give him a feather bed to fall back on, he'll go on relying on it. I can understand that you want him to have a safety net in case he crashes, but if he wasn't so sure you would always be there he would be a damned sight more sensible.'

Susanna kept her eyes down. She was busy making sure she did not involuntarily catch Niall Ardrey's eye again. She had no idea where he was sitting, but until she was in her own seat she would not feel safe, and she only listened to Johnny with partial attention.

He gave a sigh. 'Okay, lecture over. It's your life and I'll keep my mouth shut about how you run it. Forget I said anything.'

She sank into her seat with a sense of relief, then looked round at Johnny, realising what he had said and sorry that she had not responded. Giving him a warm smile she said: 'You're probably right, Johnny, but he is my brother.'

Johnny put a hand on top of hers, kissing the top of her head lightly. 'I know. Blood's thicker than water and all that jazz. I have two sisters myself, you know, I see as little of them as possible; they're both incredibly bossy and have one track minds.'

She laughed. 'What track is that?'

'They both want to get me married off—it drives them crazy to see me so happy when I'm single. Their idea of a caring relationship is to set up blind dates for me with the most boring, ugly girls they can find.'

'Poor Johnny.' The lights began to dim again and Johnny settled down to enjoy the second act, smiling, Susanna studied his profile out of the corner of her eyes. Johnny's confession that he had had a disastrous love affair when he was very young had given her new insights into his character. She sensed that he would never give all of himself to anyone again; he had learnt caution too early and the lesson had been imprinted indelibly on his memory.

Her own experience was quite different. She had never been through any traumatic emotional storms. She had a sunny, happy childhood behind her and she had grown up knowing exactly what she wanted to do with her life. Her success was early and showed no signs of diminishing; she could work to her own time-table and had more than enough money for her very moderate needs. She had never met anyone who made her feel, as Alex had said Sîan made him feel, that she could spend the rest of her life with him. The truth was that she had never felt that she needed a man sharing her whole life. She was too busy and too content with things as they were.

She had always had friends among the opposite sex, she liked their company when she wasn't working, but she certainly did not yet want to alter any part of her world to accommodate a husband. She knew what that would involve, she had seen her schoolfriends marry and have babies, give up jobs and careers and settle for a domestic life. That was not for Susanna. She enjoyed playing with babies but she felt no overriding need to have one of her own. Or, at least, not yet. She might want one some time in the dim and distant future, she might even decide to marry, but she had no intention whatever of giving up her work. It was a vital part of her; she felt more fully alive when she was working than she did at any other time. She did the housework in her flat out of a sense of necessity; she liked living in a tidy environment and someone had to do it. She enjoyed cooking; it was a creative activity, like gardening; you could play around with colour and scent to make pleasing combinations. But the idea of being immersed in domestic work all day long every day of the year was an appalling one to her. It would leave too much of her uninvolved.

I'd suffocate, she thought, staring vaguely at the stage, then a line in the play got through to her and she laughed aloud and forgot everything else in the enjoyment of Shaw's wit.

When they left the theatre they found the streets crowded with people who had also been to see a play. Cars crawled along in nose to tail lines and they had to dart across the street rapidly to get to the restaurant where they were having an after-theatre supper.

'Have you booked, sir?' the head waiter asked as they waited in the bar.

'Yes, the name's Hendrix.'

'Hendrix . . . yes, sir, may I take your coats?' He took them, handed them to a cloakroom girl and waved them to a table in the small bar. 'Perhaps you would like to have a drink while you study the menu?' As they sat down he placed a leather-bound menu in front of each of them, bowed and withdrew leaving them to order their drinks from the bar waiter.

'Hungry?' Johnny asked and Susanna shook her head.

'I won't sleep tonight if I eat much, I'll just have a light meal.' She chose melon and parma ham followed by a plain omelette and salad, and Johnny made a wry face.

'I never get to sleep until the early hours

anyway, so eating late doesn't bother me.' He led a
bohemian existence, never keeping regular hours,
although he still seemed to produce an incredible
volume of work. Susanna often wondered when he
did it; he always seemed ready to drop whatever he
was doing and go off to a party or drive into the
country for the day. He described himself
cheerfully as a committed insomniac and it did
seem to be a way of life; he presumably did a great
deal of his work during the night when most
sensible people are fast asleep in bed.

The head waiter returned and took Susanna's
order, then turned to Johnny who gave him a
cheerful smile. 'I'm going to be more adventurous.
I'll start with that delicious prawn dish you do, the
one in garlic sauce; then I'll have Scallopina
Marsala with saffron rice. Can I see the wine list?
Thanks. Let's see . . . have you got a nice Chianti?
Yes, that one will do, number thirty two. Just one
bottle, my companion will barely drink a glass of
it and I'm driving tonight.'

When the man had gone Susanna said teasingly:
'I'd better drink more than one glass if you've
ordered a bottle. You had a couple of drinks
before we went to the theatre.'

'Watching my intake? You sound like a wife,
you'd better watch it,' Johnny said and he was not
altogether joking, his eyes were sharp.

Susanna grimaced. 'Sorry, it must be the effect
of Shaw.'

'You've never seen me drunk,' Johnny said,
aggressively.

'I know, I said I was sorry.'

'I used to get drunk when I was about twenty; it
seemed a very sophisticated thing to do then, I

thought I was a real man, staggering about and throwing up. It didn't take long for me to decide I hated myself next morning and it was a damned stupid way of carrying on. I know exactly how much I can drink now, and I never go over my limit. I like to have a good time and that doesn't involve getting drunk.' He stopped dead, a startled look on his face. 'My God, I'm doing it again. . . .'

'What?' Susanna asked, baffled.

'Lecturing you—that's the second time tonight. I'd better look out, hadn't I? I must be getting old.' He finished his drink, frowning. 'Or maybe it's this stuff I'm turning out for TV. I've got so used to writing dialogue with conflict in it that I've started talking like my own scripts.'

'I meant to say—I saw last night's episode and I thought it was terrific. I was really gripped.' Susanna picked up a peanut from the bowl on the table between them. Johnny looked complacent.

'It wasn't bad, was it? Mind you, Roy Osmond really mangled his lines. Said he couldn't say what I'd written, it didn't sound like his character. I told him: look, chum, just try a bit of acting, that's what you're paid for, isn't it? I'm paid for the difficult stuff like thinking, leave that to me. He didn't like it. . . .'

His voice faded into the background for Susanna as she stared across the small bar. Niall Ardrey had just walked in behind the girl she had seen at his house the night she took Sian's compact back. She looked utterly ravishing in a black silk evening cape trimmed with a silk fringe at the hem; it was either a brilliant copy of a 1920s' costume or the real thing in which case it must have cost a fortune. Clothes of that period were valuable antiques now and much sought after, particularly when they were as good as that. The head waiter was rushing forward to greet them.

Susanna watched as he reverently received the cape over his outstretched arm and slid it deftly to his hovering assistant. Niall was in evening clothes, too. Susanna had not even noticed that when she saw him in the theatre, she had been too stunned to see him to take any notice of what he was wearing. The black suit made him look even taller and his skin seemed more tanned in contrast to that formal white shirt.

'Actors aren't the real bugbear, though,' Johnny said, blissfully unaware that he had lost her attention. 'Directors and producers, they're the ones who drive me right round the bend.'

What was the girl's name? Susanna thought, trying to remember. She had heard Niall speak to her. What had he called her?

'If we weren't organised we wouldn't have any chance of stopping them cutting our work to shreds; thank God for the Guild,' Johnny said.

Susanna smiled and nodded. She had heard all this before and there was nothing she could usefully contribute; it was Johnny's favourite topic of conversation, although it always became a monologue because all she did was listen while he talked.

She watched Niall and his companion walk over to a table on the other side of the intimate little bar. The girl sat down with a rustle of taffeta underskirts; she was wearing a very short dress with a deep frill at the hem, which came to her knees. It was flame-red and very eye-catching; the neckline plunging in a dramatic V-shape which revealed a good deal of smooth pale flesh on which gleamed a heart-shaped diamond pendant. The dress suited her sleek black hair and oval cameo of a face; she looked faintly Spanish, which, no doubt, was the intention.

'Your table is ready, sir,' the head waiter murmured and Susanna started. Johnny rose at once and she stood up too, carefully not letting her eyes roam to where Niall and his companion sat. Johnny put an arm round her back and steered her into the dining room, still talking.

'So then I said to them. . . .' He paused to let Susanna sit down, took his seat opposite her on the cream-leather banquette seats, and picked up again, exactly where he had left off, once they were both seated. Susanna played with a bread stick, breaking it into tiny pieces while she listened. The waiter brought their first courses and poured a little wine into their glasses and Johnny looked greedily at his prawns in their buttery garlic sauce.

'You should have had these, they're exquisite.'

'I like melon, especially in summer.'

'Good heavens—she talks,' Johnny said in exaggerated amazement. 'I was beginning to think you had been struck dumb. Forget Alex and enjoy yourself.'

Looking at him apologetically, Susanna said: 'Sorry, I was miles away.' It wasn't true, of course; she knew that her mind was concentrated on something much nearer than she cared to admit but if Johnny chose to jump to conclusions she wasn't going to disabuse him. She hadn't realised that Johnny had noticed her inattention and she couldn't blame him for being a little disgruntled.

He had, as always, been very eloquent on his favourite subject and deserved a more interested audience.

'My fault, I was talking shop,' he said honestly. 'I shouldn't do it, I tell myself so every time but. . . .'

'I know, what's on your mind comes out of your mouth,' Susanna said, laughing.

'Exactly.'

'Oh, well, I do it myself,' she said tolerantly.

'Very rarely, honey. You don't really give that much away at all, do you? I sometimes wonder what I really know about you. Oh, I don't mean day-to-day things like what you prefer to eat or what you enjoy doing in your spare time—I mean the big stuff, like what you're actually thinking about while I'm jabbering on at you about everything under the sun. Where did you get to just now? You weren't with me, that was obvious. You smile and nod and watch me with eyes that don't see me at all while you're in some other world, inside that head of yours.' He lazily forked prawns into his mouth in between sentences and his tone was gently disinterested, but Susanna felt uncomfortable. It wasn't like Johnny to probe so deeply; he always liked their talk kept light and frothy except when he began to complain about his working conditions.

'I've nearly finished the fairy story illustrations,' she said evasively. 'I'm going to miss them. I can't remember when I last had such fun doing a commission.'

'What are you doing next?' Johnny was buttering a roll, she watched his slim deft fingers absently.

'I have to go straight on to some pen-and-ink drawings for a new edition of Hardy. I'll have to go down to Dorset to find some locations and original farming implements, they have a very good collection in the Dorchester Museum, and elsewhere in the county. Dorset hasn't changed as much as other parts of Britain; you can still find corners which are the same as when Hardy lived there.'

Johnny watched the waiter remove their plates. 'I don't care much for Hardy, myself—not the novels, anyway. The style he used was archaic even when he was writing; he's so long-winded.'

'But that atmosphere! And the characters! He really has some wonderful stories, too.'

Johnny conceded the point, shrugging. 'He'd have made a damned good scriptwriter for soap opera if he could have kept the long words down a bit.'

Susanna giggled. 'Blasphemy!'

They ate their main course talking about Hardy and moved on to discussing the films which had been made from his books. Susanna was deliberately refusing to let her eyes, or her mind, wander. She did not want to know where Niall Ardrey and his girlfriend were sitting.

Over coffee, Johnny was talking about music when he suddenly stopped and said he had to go the men's room. Susanna sipped her coffee while he was gone and casually glanced about. She saw Niall Ardrey almost at once. He was sitting just two tables away, facing her. He was not looking at her as her gaze reached him but a second later he picked up his glass and his eyes lifted and met hers. Even across so much space Susanna felt the physical impact of him; antagonism / flashed between them like summer lightning, brief but violent. She looked away at once but in that fraction of time she had seen again the aggression of his body and hard bone structure, the cool intelligence of his eyes between those black lashes, the subtle strength of his mouth and the obstinate, assured jawline.

At first sight she had told herself that he was not a man, at all—he was a juggernaut, thundering down on everything in its path and crushing it unless it got out of the way. Now she knew that he was far more dangerous than that. A juggernaut has no personal appeal; except to those who use it and make money with it. Niall Ardrey undeniably had his attractions. He gave off electric sparks of pure sexuality even when you were not within touching distance. He magnetised the eyes, drawing them towards him even when you fought with every nerve not to look at him.

What frightened Susanna more than anything else was the peculiar excitement she felt every time she saw him. It was disturbing. It left her feeling weak and shaky every time, and angrily disgusted with herself, yet she found herself staring into space now, visualising his silvery grey eyes and that cool, go-to-hell mouth which she had already discovered could both hurt and coax.

'Off again?' Johnny enquired, sinking into the seat opposite.

She came back to earth, flushing. 'Sorry. Can we go, Johnny? I'm not a very good guest, am I? I think I'm tired, I've been working so hard today.'

'Let me finish my coffee, then, and we'll ask for the bill.' Johnny was always so ready to fall in with whatever you asked. She smiled at him gratefully. He was a good fifteen years older than herself although the years sat lightly on him. He had probably looked like this for a decade and would continue to do so for another one. There were no lines on his tranquil, good-humoured face, except the laughter lines around his mouth. He would age gracefully and with reluctance, one could see that already.

A moment later Johnny caught the waiter's eye and asked for the bill, paid it and guided her out of the restaurant. She avoided looking at Niall Ardrey's table although she was conscious of him watching her. His companion was talking in a high, fluting voice which was very audible, even in the crowded restaurant.

'Daddy said it wasn't good enough so they had to repay the whole price, after all if you're spending that sort of money you expect to get one that works properly, don't you?'

Susanna did not catch Niall's reply although she was listening for the deep, cool sound of his voice. The head waiter gestured for her coat, which he placed around her with a bow, and she walked out into the warm summer night without a backward glance.

She did not sleep too well that night, which was unusual, because she was not usually a poor sleeper. Her mind was too active tonight; she was very hyper-tense, flushed and restless in the bed even with just one sheet over her. There was a full moon making ghostly patterns on her bedroom wall, that might have had something to do with it. Moonlight was dangerous, everyone knew that, she reminded herself.

She was up late next morning, heavy-eyed and rather irritable, and found it hard to work. She broke for a coffee after an hour of hopeless struggle and sat in the kitchen sipping the black liquid with her eyes shut. She had taken some pills but her head still ached. What she needed was some sleep. At the moment every tiny noise made her jump.

The door bell rang and she did jump, about a foot in the air, her coffee splashing all over the place.

She put it down shakily and went out, rubbing the damp patch on her jeans where the coffee had stained them, crossly grimacing.

Pulling open the door she gave her brother a surprised look. 'Oh, hallo, Alex. What are you doing here? Why aren't you at work?'

'I've got migraine,' Alex said, walking past her with a surprisingly cheerful expression for someone who was supposed to be ill.

She closed the door. 'Migraine? I didn't know you got that—has it cleared up now?' He was wearing his best suit, she saw in bewilderment, and his favourite shirt, a smooth pale blue one with a stiff white collar.

'I had it so that I could go to an interview,' Alex said, flinging himself down on the couch in her sitting room with his hands behind his head.

'How amoral of you.' She did a double-take, realising what he had said. 'Interview for what?'

'A job, of course.' He hadn't looked this happy for weeks and Susanna sat down next to him slowly, staring at him, as he propped his legs on the coffee table.

'And you got it?' He had to have got the job, or

he wouldn't look as if the sun had just come up again in his sky. He was grinning broadly as he loosened his tie.

'I got it,' he said exultantly. 'I can give in my notice now and stop working for that swine Niall Ardrey. I can't wait to know that I don't get my money from him. Everything I've eaten has been choking me for weeks, just thinking that I owed my very bread to him. And it's promotion, too— I'll be earning more and having more responsibility,' He took off his tie and opened the collar of his shirt. 'Isn't it terrific?'

'Terrific, I'm very glad for you,' Susanna said, smiling at him with a relief which almost dispelled the headache she had had all morning. 'Let's celebrate by going out to lunch somewhere special. I'll buy us some champagne. I'll have to change into something more suitable, I won't be long.' She paused, then looked back over her shoulder and said severely: 'And take your damned feet off my coffee table!'

CHAPTER FIVE

SUSANNA'S schedule for the following month had to be re-arranged because the author of the Hardy book had not finished the text. He was, the publisher admitted with obvious irritation, barely half-way through it, and until they saw the whole manuscript there was little point in making a final decision on the illustrations.

'Sorry, I know it's a bind and I promise we'll get the man to put a move on, but I think it's essential that you have a copy of the final text before you start working on your drawings.'

'I've already booked into hotels in Dorset,' Susanna said, frowning. 'I'll have to cancel and re-book later. What a nuisance, a massive waste of my time, not to mention money.'

'Send us a list of your expenses,' the publisher said reluctantly, shifting on his chair with a wary expression.

'I don't know if I can fit it in later. I have a string of other jobs to do and some of them can't be re-arranged. Maybe you'd better get someone else when the writer finally delivers the text.' Susanna got up without haste, expecting the reply which came hurriedly.

'No, no, we don't want to do that, Susanna. We have a very high opinion of your work, you know that.'

'Couldn't you get anyone else for the money?' Susanna asked and he winced.

'That's very unkind.' He gave her a lachrymose smile; he was a very thin man with pale brown, straw-like hair which was thatched stiffly on the top of his slightly pointed head. His face was gaunt; almost spectral, it was rumoured, from years of anxiety about the profitability of his firm. His eyes had a fixed stare, perhaps because he constantly gazed at the advance of bankruptcy. He was, nevertheless, an extraordinarily good publisher whose firm had produced a long list of highly respected books, none of them in the bestseller class, but all of them unusual. It was that difference in the books he published which made him a man Susanna—and many others—enjoyed working with, despite the fact that every single penny had to be wrung out of him to cries of agony which often made sensitive writers give up in the face of such pain.

'This is a most unusual book—the idea is so fascinating, a serious study of the society which produced Hardy—we want to have the right artist to match this writer. Photographs ... we considered them, fascinating too, of course, we may well have some as well as your drawings but they wouldn't give the book the right feel. Old photographs are static, we want some illustrations which bring the period alive.'

'I know, you told me all this long ago,' Susanna said. 'Don't try to sell me on the idea again, Robin. I didn't say I didn't want to do the book— I said it was a nuisance having to put the work off when I'm ready to start it.'

'Of course, quite understood, very annoying, I'll pass on what you say to the writer. Tiresome man, doesn't answer letters, isn't on the phone. . . .'

'He sounds very sensible to me,' Susanna said as he wafted her to the door with an appealing smile.

'The trouble with publishing is writers,' Robin said. 'A pity, there you are, we have to have them. We'll let you know the instant we see the text. . . .'

The door closed. Susanna almost heard the sigh of relief with which he scuttled back to his chair. She made a gruesome face at his secretary who winked at her, and as Susanna walked out of the office got up and went to take dictation with a shorthand pad clutched in her hand.

Summer was having a last fling; the London air was clear and brilliant, the sky a pure cloudless blue and the sunshine hot enough to be soporific but not uncomfortably so. It wasn't a day for working, it was a day for lying on a beach or in a garden, sunbathing and relaxing. That was what Alex would be doing now; he had taken his annual leave and gone to Spain on a cut-price package tour, on impulse. He had left the agency which Niall Ardrey owned and when he came back from holiday would be starting in his new job. Susanna had driven him to Gatwick airport four days ago and promised to pick him up again when he returned.

She was, temporarily, unemployed herself; since she had completed her last job and would not now be going down to Dorset to start on the next one. She was not worried about money, she had more than enough in the bank, in her current account, to last for the next couple of months and she could always draw on her savings which she deposited to earn interest with a building society.

She thought of Alex as she was making her way home; a holiday was just what he needed, somewhere gay and sunny. She needed a holiday herself, come to that, but she didn't feel like going abroad. The cottage? she thought, frowning. It might not be a bad idea to go down there and redecorate. It certainly needed it and if she did it herself she wouldn't have the expense of calling in a professional who might charge the earth. She could kill two birds with one stone; an idea that appealed to Susanna's down-to-earth character. She could paint and wallpaper in the morning, when it wasn't so warm, and spend the afternoon lazing about in the garden getting a tan.

She felt more able to relax now that Alex was getting over Sîan. It would still take time for him to forget her completely, but he was no longer so morose and silent. He was forcing himself to break out of that dull, dead misery, thank God.

That evening she had dinner with some married friends. Isobel had been at school with her and they had kept in touch infrequently; neither of them ever mentioning the fact that Isobel had married Susanna's first boyfriend. Susanna didn't mention it because she thought George rather boring now and was afraid to offend Isobel. Isobel didn't mention it because she was worried in case Susanna regretted having let George slip through her fingers. She was under the impression that Susanna didn't know this, but her guilty, apologetic manner whenever she was with Susanna had long ago made her feelings plain. Susanna was fond of Isobel; in the way one can be fond of a family joke that long ago ceased to have any impact but which is repeated through sheer habit. They had known each other since they were five. It was a long time and they didn't have to bother to be over polite to each other, but they really had little in common any more except the past.

The real reason Susanna visited Isobel was to see Emily, Isobel's three-year-old daughter and Susanna's one and only godchild. Emily was a diminutive and chatty version of her mother and Susanna adored her.

'So Alex has changed jobs again, has he?' grunted George disapprovingly as he refilled Susanna's glass at dinner. 'What's the matter with him? He'll never get on that way. Wasn't he working for Houghton, Elks and Thingummy? Big firm, that; he could have done well for himself if he'd stayed there.' George was a stockbroker; he had a tidy mind and a symmetrically arranged life, a place for everything and everything in its place, including his wife, who would not have dreamt of getting a job or arguing with any decision George ever made for both of them.

'He has a better job now,' Susanna said, sipping the Chablis with appreciation.

'Really?' George said incredulously, then snorted, examining the fish he was eating with distaste. 'Bones! Isobel—there are bones in this! I thought I told you to get fillets. Can't you get anything right?'

Agitated, Isobel peered at her own fish. 'The fishmonger swore. . . .'

'Fishmongers? They'll say anything.' George accusingly arranged a neat line of tiny bones on the side of his plate. 'Look at that! Could choke to death on them. Where was I? Oh, yes, Houghton, Whats' it and Thingummy . . . one of Ardrey's companies, aren't they? Clever fellow, Ardrey—his shares have been rising for over a year. Must have made a killing. I wonder if it's true that he's going to marry Oliver Hardwick's girl—what's her name? Jean? No, Jill.' He paused and disinterred some more tiny bones. 'Really, Isobel!

'I'm so sorry, George, I can't understand it,' Isobel said uneasily, forcing a smile for Susanna who smiled back impatiently.

'He's been seeing a lot of her lately but then she isn't the first to have hopes in that quarter and he's always wriggled off the hook before. I know her parents slightly; father daft as a brush, mother at that time of life, going around dressed up like a teenager. Ridiculous, making a fool of herself. Plenty of money, of course, but I wouldn't have said enough to interest Ardrey. Mind you; attractive girl, plenty of character. He may not get away this time.' George seemed pleased by that idea. He said it again. 'No, this time he may not get away.'

When Susanna helped her stack the dishwasher later, Isobel said: 'I'm sorry George was so cross, he hates it when little things go wrong. He's very sensitive.' Susanna looked at her with incredulity. Did she really believe that? The men her friends had married had helped to reinforce her own reluctance ever to marry unless she was lucky enough to find someone like-minded enough to live with for a lifetime. She would never have the patience to put up with George. His petty complaints and hassle over dinner would have driven her crazy.

'Don't you get bored living alone in London?' Isobel asked as she washed her hands. 'I'd hate it. I'd be frightened, in a flat, all by myself night after night.'

'What makes you think I am?' Susanna asked mischievously and walked out leaving Isobel with a stunned and horrified expression, which was, at the same time, fascinated.

'Susanna ... are you ... do you....' she babbled, pursuing her, but Susanna only laughed and refused to answer. She got rather tired at times of Isobel's complacent belief that marriage was the only way to live. Isobel had married almost straight from school, taking the first guy who asked her. She seemed busy and contented enough with her home and possessions, her child and her various friends and relations. She belonged to clubs and gardened, and read in a desultory fashion, usually the latest fat bestselling paperback or some coffee-table book which was more pictures than text. Susanna never tried to talk Isobel into discontent with her life. Why did Isobel never cease to imply that Susanna's way of living was a poor substitute for marriage?

She thought of the conversation as she was driving down to Sussex a few days later; her car laden down with buckets and mops, paint, wallpaper and brushes; everything she thought she might need to redecorate the cottage.

A wicked glint showed in her eyes. Isobel had been dying of curiosity for the rest of the evening after Susanna dropped her bombshell. It had been naughty to tease her but Susanna hadn't been able to help it. She had been irritated by George; not least because he had mentioned Niall Ardrey, not Susanna's favourite topic of conversation. Susanna didn't care who Niall Ardrey married, she didn't want to talk about him, or his future bride. Jill. Yes, that had been the girl's name, and Sussana could see why George approved of her, Jill was his type of woman. She wouldn't let the fishmonger get away with unfilleted fillets. No doubt she wouldn't let Niall Ardrey get away with much, either. It wouldn't be a marriage; more a tug of war. Susanna hoped Jill would win—she would like to see Niall Ardrey get beaten by someone.

Any day now it would be autumn; the trees had begun to lose that vivid green of summer and were slowly beginning to show the odd bronze leaf. Susanna involuntarily used her eyes all the time to absorb colour and line, shape and structure; she had long ago learnt to look below the surface of everything she saw for the internal structure which shaped it and in some ways she carried that probing curiosity through into the way she looked at the people around her. Anatomy had been one of her favourite subjects when she was at art school; she found a calm logic and a poignant fascination in the human skeleton. It was so smoothly dove-tailed and jointed, each bone fitting exactly in its place and each with its own function and movement. There was a deep satisfaction in studying it, but beyond that there was the sadness of remembering that it had once been clothed in flesh, had moved and spoken, made love and suffered, been beautiful on the surface as it was now when it was naked bone. Until you understood the human skeleton you did not understand the motion of the living creature.

When she first met Niall Ardrey she had been taken aback by his height and the breadth of shoulder, length of leg, which made him so formidable. His skeleton would be a beauty, she thought, changing gear and smiling to herself.

Although he was so powerful he had almost perfect proportion; his hips were slim and his chest muscular rather than merely large. He was a very healthy specimen; beneath that smooth brown skin lay firm muscle and she already had the impression that his mind was just as formidable and muscled.

She suddenly frowned, catching herself thinking about him. What was he doing in her head again? Every time she forgot to keep the door of her mind closed to him, he wandered in as though he had a perfect right there. His image had the same arrogant self-assurance as the man himself, no matter what you did it forced its way in.

She spent the whole of the next day scrubbing down the surfaces she meant to repaint, stripping off wallpaper and washing the ceiling. She started early in the morning and did not stop work until gone seven by which time it was almost dark. She broke for lunch briefly but only had a crisp local apple and a small slice of Wensleydale cheese followed by a cup of coffee. It was a meal she often ate when she was working hard; it saved time and trouble.

With a hand to her aching back and a faint headache she went upstairs to take a bath before getting herself an evening meal. It was marvellous to lean back in warm, scented water and relax, clearing her mind. She wriggled her pink toes, gazing at them through half-closed eyes, feeling oddly pleased with herself for having done so much. She was accustomed to working hard at her drawing and painting, but manual work was not something she often did. Attacking the stubborn wallpaper she had felt a strong satisfaction in watching it give way and peel off. It was not the same feeling one got when one finished a difficult picture, but it had been fun and had drained away some of the strange tension she had been feeling lately.

When the water began to get cold she climbed out, reluctantly, towelled herself and put on a loose kaftan which she had bought in Constantinople several years ago. It was soft and flowing velvet, embroidered in silver on the neck and hemline. Susanna brushed her damp hair back from her face and went downstairs, suddenly hungry.

She had brought down a few tins and there was a well-stocked deep freeze in the kitchen, but she was too tired to cook anything elaborate so she settled for tomato soup and toast.

She had just finished eating when she heard a sound outside on the path, the grate of a heel. Susanna sat still, listening tensely. Was she imagining it?

A moment later someone knocked firmly on the door. She looked at her watch. It was almost nine o'clock. Who on earth could be calling at this hour? Perhaps someone in the village had driven past, seen her lights and been startled into investigating? The cottage was so often empty, it might look suspicious and the local people knew that she and Alex were mostly in London, they were aware of everything that happened around here.

She opened the door cautiously, ready to slam it again if she didn't like the look of whoever stood on the step. For a second she almost did slam it when she saw Niall Ardrey. Shock made her stammer.

'W . . . what are you doing here?'

'Sorry, did I alarm you?'

He sounded suspiciously polite. Susanna peered at him, keeping the door half closed but trying at the same time to stay out of his view because she was only wearing the old kaftan. Why did he always catch her unawares?

'Do you know what time it is?'

He made a point of consulting his watch. 'Ten to nine.' Looking up again with a quizzical expression, he added: 'You don't go to bed this early, do you?'

'I wasn't expecting visitors. What do you want?'

'To talk to you?' he suggested, raising his brows.

'How did you know I was here?'

'I went round to your flat this afternoon and one of your neighbours said you had gone down to the country.'

Susanna sighed in resignation. You couldn't keep anything secret, even in a busy London block of flats. 'Which neighbour?'

'The one with the umbrella with a steel handle,' Niall said. 'She held it pointedly while she spoke to me—I got the idea she was ready to defend her honour if I tried to attack her.'

Susanna laughed. 'Oh, Miss Ervine. Well, she lives in hope.'

He laughed. 'You can be a little cat, can't you? Are you going to insist that we have this conversation out here? Aren't you suitably dressed?' He shifted his stance so that he could see more of her, and Susanna fought against an impulse to duck out of sight. Why should she hide from him? And why on earth should she want to? She had always prided herself on her strong-minded attitude to the opposite sex; it was maddening that Niall Ardrey seemed to have such a disastrous effect on her.

'Very Oriental,' he approved of the kaftan, running a lazy gaze over it which absurdly made her feel as though there was nothing hidden from him, he was aware of every curve and angle of her body in spite of the all-enveloping velvet covering her from neck to toe. 'Did you buy it in London or. . . .'

'Turkey,' she muttered.

'Oh? Which part?'

'Constantinople. I was on a cruise and we docked there for a day.' He seemed happy to lounge there on the doorstep, idly chatting. What was he doing here?

'Did you like it? I've visited Turkey a number of times, a wonderful place.'

'I'm sure you loved it, the men there seem to be your type,' Susanna said with a bite. 'The mosques are beautiful, especially The Blue Mosque, I've never seen anything like the strange blue light which seems to fill it; very cold, very remote. It's the colour of a winter dawn.' She stopped, flushing, as she realised that she had been talking the way she would to Johnny or one of her friends. They talked that way themselves but Niall Ardrey didn't come from their world, he didn't deal in ideas or beauty, he was one of the money-makers and probably laughed at talk of art.

He didn't seem to be laughing, though. He was watching her intently, his eyes far too perceptive, as though he was curious about her.

'I like the silver embroidery,' he said, putting out a hand and stroking a long index finger over the embroidery on the cuff of her sleeve.

Susanna fell back instinctively, on a reflex action, snatching the sleeve from his grasp, and he advanced. A second later the front door had shut and he was inside the cottage while she blinked in surprise and wondered how that had happened. Before she could demand that he leave, he asked: 'Is your brother here?' and at once she was bristling again.

'No, he isn't. He's in Spain on holiday before he takes up his new job.' She glared at him. 'He's left your firm—I suppose you know that? He resigned, he didn't wait for you to sack him, and he had no trouble getting another job. Alex is very talented, he's going to be very successful one day.'

He smiled at her with what in another man she might have taken for warmth, even tenderness, but it couldn't be either in Niall Ardrey, it must be sarcasm.

'You're very loyal to him, I hope he appreciates it.' Before she could answer he turned and wandered into the kitchen and looked at the table on which lay the evidences of her meal, and the book she had been reading as she ate. Niall bent over and picked it up, flipping over the pages rapidly.

'Hardy? Do you like him?'

'Yes,' she said defiantly and he looked up to eye her with mockery.

'Why do you always take every question as an attack?'

'With you it often is; what are you doing here, Mr Ardrey?'

'Niall,' he said. 'I like Hardy too, Susanna, especially this one—did you see the film? I thought it was a little slow-moving but the photography was beautiful.'

She took the bowl and spoon from the table and dumped them in the sink. 'I'm very tired, Mr Ardrey, I've been redecorating all day and I'm dead on my feet. Can you get to the point?'

He put down the book and moved to survey her, his mouth crooked. 'You're not worried about the usual conventions, are you?'

Susanna stiffened warily. 'What does that mean?' It sounded oddly like the lead-up to some sort of pass and she felt her nerves prickling with tension.

'I mean that you never bother to be polite,' he said, then his eyes mocked her. 'Now I wonder what you thought I meant?'

Her cheeks burnt, and she looked down because she did not want those lucid grey eyes probing her face and reading thoughts she struggled to evict from her mind. She did not want to like him or be aware of him; she didn't want to notice that he was wearing black jeans which looked beautifully cut and styled by some very expensive designer, she suspected. He wore them with a white shirt and a black cashmere sweater which clung to his powerful chest and slim waist like a second skin. Her eyes didn't linger yet she still absorbed everything about the way he looked and it was disturbing and ridiculous to be this aware of any man.

'You've been redecorating?' he asked, looking around the kitchen then walked out and stood in the doorway of the sitting room which echoed oddly with the sound of his voice when he spoke. It was empty and clean, the walls bare plaster now and the curtainless windows looking blank and menacing with the night which pressed against them. 'When did you start? Did you do all this?'

'Yes,' she said, standing just behind him and tight-lipped with impatience. She wanted him to go, every second that he stayed here seemed to be pulsing with menace, Susanna was afraid of him, of what he might do to her. She didn't want to get involved with him. He could hurt her. She felt like someone safely drifting in a transparent but protective balloon, high above the earth, so that she could see and hear everything that went on below her without being in any danger of being dragged into contact. Niall Ardrey could pierce that fine, fragile balloon and she would go tumbling and crashing down to earth.

'Susanna?' His voice startled her, she had been so intent on her picture of the balloon and herself falling out of it, smiling to herself as she decided to do a quick sketch of it before she went up to bed, that she had forgotten he was there and had a queer little jerk of shock at hearing him use her name.

'You aren't listening,' he accused and he was so close that her eyes stretched open wide, her pupils dilating. 'Your hair's the most unusual colour I've ever seen,' he murmured. 'Neither brown nor red.' He touched a long, curling tendril of it and she flinched. 'It's full of electricity, isn't it? I can almost see the sparks.' His hand stroked down from the crown of her head to where the strands clustered on her shoulder. 'I can feel them tingling on my skin,' he said and she swallowed, her throat

suddenly raw as though she had a sore throat and
a cold coming.

'You still haven't told me why you're here,' she
said in a dry voice.

'What do you wash it with? Lemons? It seems to
smell of them.' He bent his head and with disbelief
she felt the touch of his cheek against her hair. 'It's
like silk,' he said, his voice muffled as though he
was talking into her hair. 'My grandmother wants
to meet you. Sîan never stops talking about you, it
seems. She can't talk about Alex, I suppose, so she
talks about you, and my grandmother would like
you to have lunch with her.'

'I'm sorry,' Susanna said huskily, stepping away
from him and walking back into the kitchen. He
followed and she said over her shoulder: 'As you
can see, I'm very busy and I won't be coming back
to London for several weeks. I'm afraid I won't be
able to have lunch with your grandmother.'

'She doesn't live in London. She lives in
Brighton, just a few miles from here. Surely you
can spare a couple of hours? Sîan hasn't many
friends. She's rather lonely.'

'I'm hardly her age group!' Susanna protested.
'She must have friends of her own age! Or haven't
you let her make any friends?'

He ran a hand over his vital black hair with an
impatient gesture. 'Good heavens, is that something else you blame me for? I haven't stopped
Sîan from making friends. I had to send her to a
boarding school. What else could I do? When her
mother died she was only eight. I couldn't look
after her. I was out all day, I often had to go
abroad for a week at a time—that was no sort of
home life for a little girl, and the shock of her

mother's death had made my grandmother ill. She had a heart attack a week after the funeral, I thought she was doing to die, too. I couldn't leave Sîan with her, either, even when she was allowed home from the hospital. It would have been too much for her, there was no question of that. I had no choice. Sîan had to go away to school and she always spent the holidays at Brighton or at my mother's old home in the country.'

'But not with you?' Susanna said drily and he frowned.

'I've told you. . . .'

'I know—you were too busy and too important to take time off just to be with your little sister. I understand, perfectly, Mr Ardrey.' She gave him a cool, bland smile and he fumed under it, his black brows jerking together.

'It wasn't the way you make it sound. Of course I was with Sîan from time to time. I took her to Greece with me one year, for three weeks. I took her to Scotland another time and I always spent Christmas with her and my grandmother, I never missed a year. I visited her at school at weekends, too. I don't know what sort of impression she's given you but I'm not a cold-hearted monster!'

'You say that with real feeling,' Susanna mocked and his face ran with angry blood. The next second he had caught her head between his hands, his palms cool against her warm skin, and Susanna looked up at him, startled, and too taken by surprise to pull away. He stared at her insistently, as though he was memorising every detail of her face, and she felt that long, fixed stare as a physical contact, making her pulses leap and flicker with disturbed fire.

'Does it always have to be a shouting match every time I see you?' he asked harshly.

She opened her mouth to answer and he muttered abruptly: 'No, don't say anything. Just let me kiss you.' He bent his head and his mouth touched hers. Susanna stood, frozen in shock, her eyes still wide open and able to see that Niall's eyes had closed, his cheekbones and jawline were tense with a feeling she could experience in the fierce pressure of his lips as they moved against hers, in the way his fingers ran up into her hair, winding tendrils of it through each parted finger, and the sound of his rapid, jerky breathing.

Susanna was suddenly cold. She was not the type who fainted normally but she had done so once or twice as a child and she recognised the chill on the back of her neck, the drowning sensation making her legs weak and her mouth dry. Her own eyes closed and she sagged against him, grasping his sweater, admitting with dismay that she needed that hungry contact, mouth to mouth, the urgent pressure of their bodies, as she had never needed anything before. Her mind might recoil from the idea, but it could not argue with the deepest instincts of the body.

Desire was running through her in a tidal rush which swept away all wish to think, nothing seemed to matter but the satisfaction of this painful hunger; her hands trembled as they touched his wide shoulders and moved inwards to the smooth flesh of his throat. She felt a heavy pulse beating at the base of it and Niall gave a stifled groan as her fingers explored. His hands were moving downward, flattening the velvet of the kaftan so that the shape of the flesh beneath it clung to his palms as he moulded her like a sculptor, blindly discovering her body without looking at her, shaping her breasts in the cup of his hands, caressing the inward curve of her waist, following the flow of her hips and thighs. She was hidden beneath the velvet yet his hands made her naked, and she gave a deep moan of intense excitement.

Niall buried his face in the side of her neck, his lips hot, pressing into her warm flesh and forcing back her head. 'I want you,' he whispered shakily and for a fraction of time she was in profound shock, aching with aroused blood.

She almost surrendered, gave herself without any attempt at resistance. Her lips moved to say: 'Yes.' She felt them silently open, her tongue had the groaned assent ready, then she forced herself back from this dazed weakness, breathing rawly, and pulled away, her eyes forced open. She had to push Niall to make him let her go and he stared at her with eyes which glittered like black stars, their pupils so dilated that they seemed to have taken over the whole iris. His skin was hot and he was as breathless as Susanna, she heard the rapid intake of his lungs.

'No,' she said. It was almost a groan, harsh and low. It was a victory which tasted strangely of defeat; it was not what she had wanted to say but what she had to say. She had said it often enough before to other men and never with any difficulty; this was the first time she had ever said: 'No' and meant the opposite.

Niall gave a strange, wry smile. 'I know—it's crazy, do you think I haven't told myself that a hundred times? You're impossible; whenever I see

you we end up quarrelling, half the time I feel I
want to strangle you.' He looked into her eyes and
her heart seemed to crash into her ribs. It was an
illusion, of course, she told herself; hearts don't
bang about inside you and you can't be deafened
by the sound of your own heart beating. 'The
other half of the time I want to do something very
different,' he said huskily.

What is the matter with me? Susanna thought. I
have all the classic symptoms of a disease I don't
believe in! She had never believed that anyone fell
in love—they just convinced themselves that they
had because the fantasy was a useful way of
forming a bond from which children would result.
Susanna had often spent hours studying birds and
animals. If you were going to draw them you had
to understand them; not merely in the physical
sense of how the muscle ran under the flesh and
how they moved and fed, but in terms of their
behaviour patterns, what each species did and
why. She felt you could learn a lot about human
beings from watching animals; not least as far as
mating rituals went. Remembering the way her
mother had given her whole life to loving and
caring first for her delicate husband and then for
Alex, Susanna had felt no impulse to do the same
for any man. The pattern held for all her married
friends, as far as she could see; they gave
themselves up to home-making and child-rearing
and even those who went on with a job seemed
more obsessed with their home life than their
career. Love demanded too much; it wasn't
satisfied with anything less than totality. There
might be a man somewhere who wouldn't be so
devouring, but Susanna's intelligence warned her

that it wouldn't be Niall Ardrey. One look at that hard bone structure, those insistent grey eyes, told you that he was a taker; he would want everything he could get of you, he wouldn't accept half measures.

'Nothing to say?' he asked after a long pause during which he had watched her intently. 'That's a first for you; you usually have a great deal to say—why are you so quiet now?' His voice was calmer, more in control, the dark flush had receded from his face and his body had slackened from the terrifying tension which had held it a moment ago. Susanna felt herself shivering; as though she was bitterly cold now that the aching heat had left her body.

'There doesn't seem much to say. It wouldn't work and we both know it, and I don't want to get into something that can only end badly.' She gave him a stiff smile. 'You'd better go while we're both sane.'

He shrugged, his mouth wry. 'I suppose you're right. Sex is an explosive game even when the players know what they're doing, and I sure as hell don't know what I'm doing now. I didn't come here intending that to happen. You just get to me, maybe because you make me so damn mad. My temperature shoots sky high when you're looking at me with that go-to-hell stare, I start wanting to. . . .' he broke off, grimacing. 'Well, you know what I want to do. I'm male and my instincts aren't always rational.'

'Male instincts rarely are,' Susanna said with cold sarcasm. 'Goodnight, Mr Ardrey.' She walked out to the front door and he followed more slowly.

'Mr Ardrey?' he repeated drily. 'Now you're being ridiculous. After kissing me like that . . .'

'It seems safer to be formal,' she retorted, opening the door.

He gave her a mocking little bow. 'Very well, Miss Howard. You still haven't told me if you'll have lunch with my grandmother and, before you ask, I won't be there, I'll stay well out of the way. You can see her and Sîan quite safely.'

She flushed, hesitated then shrugged. 'Oh, very well. What's the address and what time should I be there?' After all, what harm could it do to meet his grandmother? Come to that, she would like to see Sîan again even though she was angry with her for hurting Alex.

CHAPTER SIX

At exactly twelve-thirty next day, Susanna parked
outside the address Niall had given her. She liked
to be punctual—it was the habit of a lifetime,
acquired like so many other good habits, as a way
of making sure she did not ever need to rely on
anybody else. When she was a child, her mother
had always been too busy to bother about
Susanna, she had had to take care of herself. In
their home it was understood that men needed to
be waited on from morning to night, but females
of any age were tough and could stand up to
anything. Susanna had, willy-nilly, learnt self-
sufficiency very early. As a child she could
remember being ashamed of her own health and
vigour, the energy and drive that made her father
smile and call her 'my sturdy little pony'. She had
sometimes wished she, too, was frail and helpless,
at times she envied Alex because he got so much
attention. She learnt to take care of herself,
though; she worked hard at school and later at
college, she was neat and careful and fiercely self-
sufficient, although she could not help wondering
if self-sufficiency was all it was cracked up to be—a
little leaning on someone might be nice for a
change, she occasionally thought. Only for a
minute, then she got on with life because Susanna
was a well-trained realist, getting on with living
was what she had learnt as a small child.

She was curious about Niall Ardrey's grand-

mother and looked up at the perfect Regency
façade of her tiny terraced house before she got
out of the car, wondering if the exterior of the
house would give her any clues about its owner.
As she looked, Susanna's mouth parted in a
delighted gasp. It was a dolls' house; sugar-candy
pink and white, with rounded bay windows hung
with striped pink and white brocade curtains, a
rosy pink tiled roof and a panelled white front
door with a cherub's head as a doorknocker, made
of brass, but gleaming bright gold from hours of
being lovingly polished.

All the houses in the terrace were structurally
identical, but this one stood out among the rest
because someone loved it and had given it
character. A flowerbox ran under the ground-floor
bay window; a riot of geraniums in pink and red,
blue petals of lobelia, and white bobbles of
alyssum. The steps which ran up to the front door
were stone, hollowed in the centre from years of
use, but spotlessly whitewashed. There was a
pocket handkerchief garden, with a railing around
it; it had been paved, and in the centre of the
paving stones stood a fat cherub, brother to the
one on the doorknocker, smiling mischievously
while it played a flute.

Susanna loved the house; it had slightly smug
charm, rather like that of a very good little girl, in
a poke bonnet, who has freckles across her nose
and a wicked glint in her eye in spite of her demure
air.

Susanna got out of her car, went up the three
steps, fitting her feet precisely into the worn dip in
the stone, and carefully lifted the cherub's head. It
had pleated wings folded above it, like a miniature

tent, and its plump hands were clasped together piously.

'Sorry to disturb your prayers,' Susanna said to it as she knocked twice. 'This is a most undignified way to treat a cherub, especially one busy praying.'

'Oh, don't let him fool you—he isn't praying. He's got one eye open to watch the people going past—he's just pretending to pray. He's very conceited; he loves to be admired.'

Susanna smiled at the old lady who had opened the front door. She was as tiny and demure as her house, her hair silvery, her eyes bright, her nose small and with a slight upwards tilt which had impertinence and charm. She was wearing a lavender cotton dress which reflected the faded blue of her eyes. They must once have been the same colour as Sîan's, Susanna thought.

'He's delightful; your whole house is delightful. I don't often find myself talking to doorknockers.' Susanna laughed. 'I feel I ought to explain that—I don't want you to think I go around talking to myself.'

'Oh, I do—it's often much easier than talking to people, they answer back and interrupt your thoughts, especially Niall, he seems to revel in arguments and nothing is so tiring and unproductive.' Holding out her hand she added: 'I'm Lydia Ardrey and you're Susanna—such a lovely name and it suits you. Thank you for coming to see me. I hope you like cheese?'

Bewildered, Susanna said: 'Yes, I love cheese.'

'I've made a cheese soufflé—it just went into the oven, time for you to have some sherry before lunch. Do come in, Susanna.'

The diminutive hall was papered in pink and green; impossibly beautiful apple blossom breaking from curly twigs which looked more like writhing caterpillars. An oval mirror, framed in white with a fine gilded line running along the edge, hung on one wall, reflecting some fat pink roses with golden hearts which had spilled pollen in a fine golden heap of dust around the base of the vase, into which they had been thrust without any attempt at arrangement. Susanna felt even more as if she had entered a dolls' house; the ceiling was so low and everything so small.

'Come into the parlour,' Lydia Ardrey said and Susanna couldn't resist murmuring: 'Said the spider to the fly. . . .' then gave a faint groan. 'Sorry,' she said until she saw the older woman laughing.

'Not many people use the word parlour these days, do they? A pity, I like old-fashioned things, including words. I will not call a room a "lounge" as though all one could do in it was sit about idly. I hate to see people lounging. My chairs do not allow you to lounge; they force you to sit up with a straight back.'

Susanna had followed her into the small, square room with a bulge at one end where the bay window projected out into the garden and she could see exactly what Lydia Ardrey meant. The chairs were of the same period as the house and were not meant to be sprawled in, they had straight backs and wooden arms. Sîan was sitting on a sofa covered in faded pink velvet. She got up, giving Susanna a shy, nervous nod, murmuring: 'Hallo,' and then standing there, all arms and long, slender legs, gawkily uncertain of herself.

'Will you have a glass of sherry, Susanna? Sweet or dry?' Lydia seated herself like a queen, her tiny hands clasping the arms of the chair; they were pale and had skin like fine wrinkled crêpe, the knuckles blue and protruding. Susanna had hesitated between sofa and chairs; Lydia gestured regally and Susanna obediently sat down on the sofa facing her.

'Sweet sherry, please.'

'I will have the same, Sîan dear,' Lydia announced.

Susanna glanced rapidly around the room, taking in a sketchy impression of a very old and well-trodden carpet, a few pretty pieces of porcelain standing on the two occasional tables in the room, a charming early Victorian glass clock whose internal works could be seen.

'So,' Lydia said. 'You are Alex's sister—are you like him? Is there a family resemblance? I have never met him, you know. Sîan did not see fit to bring him to see me.'

Sîan almost dropped the glass of sherry she was carefully handing to Susanna. Her fingers shook and Susanna gave her a quick, sympathetic smile.

'I didn't think. . . .' Sîan began and her grandmother softly cut her short.

'You shouldn't jump to conclusions. That is one thing you and your brother have in common, Sîan—you both tend to make up your minds before you have thought things through. Niall was far too impulsive when he was in his teens; I lived on tenterhooks wondering what he would do next. And his temper was on a very short fuse.'

'Wrong tense,' Susanna said. 'It still is!'

Mrs Ardrey looked at her, her eyes very sharp.

'Possibly so, although I haven't seen much evidence of it lately.' She took a sip of the sherry her granddaughter had just given her. 'I allow myself one glass of sherry a day; it gives me something to look forward to. Tell me, do you think Sîan has enough talent to pursue a career in art?'

Susanna was taken aback by the abrupt change of subject. 'Well, I . . . I don't know, I haven't seen any of her work.'

Sîan was very flushed. 'Oh, Grandma, I told you—it hasn't anything to do with Susanna, it was all my own idea. I told Niall, but of course he didn't listen. . . .'

'Of course, he wouldn't,' Susanna said drily.

'I'm sorry if I've caused any more problems, it never occurred to me that Niall would bother you about it.' Sîan gave Susanna a pleading, apologetic look. She was wearing a black-and-white striped cotton dress with a tight waistline; it made her look so slender you felt you could encircle her waist with two hands; the effect was oddly Edwardian, you were surprised at the hemline which came just below the knee. It should have been down at ankle level.

'Niall was being sarcastic,' she went on unsteadily. 'He said, okay, if you don't want to go to university, what *do* you want to do? And he gave me a nasty look, expecting me to say nothing, I suppose, but then I said I'd like to study art and that surprised him.' She gave a small, satisfied smile.

'When did you decide you wanted to study art?' Susanna asked and Sîan shrugged.

'There and then. I'd been thinking—what would

I really enjoy doing? And that seemed one thing. The other option was out of the question.'

Susanna could imagine what that was, she looked at Mrs Ardrey briefly without comment and Sîan saw their exchange of looks and broke out indignantly. 'No, it wasn't . . . what I mean is . . . if you must know I'd like to learn to cook.'

'To cook?' Mrs Ardrey said, putting down her glass of sherry unfinished.

'To cook?' Susanna gasped at the same moment.

Sîan looked sullen. 'You see? If I told Niall that I'd like to learn to cook he'd laugh, but I would, I used to love domestic science lessons at school and I am good at cooking, it's one of the few things I do really well, but Niall doesn't think cooking is serious. He wants to turn me into an intellectual, make me have a career, put me in the firm. He keeps saying to me: don't I want to *do* something with my life, as though getting a degree meant you had made it and life would be beautiful for ever more. I don't see it, myself. Now, cooking makes sense. Everyone has to eat and you can really enjoy doing something that has a point to it. It's useful, as well as being a lot of fun.'

'Are you saying,' Lydia Ardrey asked clearly in tones breathing impatience, 'are you telling me, Sîan, that after all you do *not* want to go to an art school?'

'I don't know what I want to do,' Sîan said, very flushed. 'I just want Niall to stop badgering me. I'm sick of being lectured and pushed around.'

There was a tap on the door and an elderly woman put her head round the door. 'Lunch is ready,' she announced and Lydia Ardrey pulled

herself to her feet; the way she moved giving
Susanna a suspicion that she was arthritic.

'Give me your arm, Sîan,' she said, holding out
her wrinkled hand, the knuckles on it blue and
stiff. Sîan reluctantly helped her to the door and
Susanna could see the resemblance between them
clearly; they were of the same build and colouring
and, judging by the portrait in Niall's house, Lydia
Ardrey must have been beautiful when she was
Sîan's age.

They ate in a room even smaller than the
parlour. It had dark oak-panelled walls, a small
oval dining table which was elaborately laid with
fine glass and old, polished silver worn with years
of use. A silver bowl of fruit took up the centre of
the table and the elderly woman served them with
halves of grapefruit whose surfaces were sprinkled
with currants and brown sugar which had been
toasted under a grill so that the crust on top of the
fruit was bubbling and hot.

'How delicious,' Susanna said, and Lydia
looked sideways at Sîan, who was pink.

'Sîan's recipe,' her grandmother said, and
Susanna congratulated her.

'Did you invent it?'

Sîan shook her head. 'I got it out of a recipe
book.' She smiled. 'But wait until you taste
Grandma's soufflé; it's mouthwatering.'

It was; perfectly cooked and with a delicious
taste and a melting texture inside which contrasted
beautifully with the firm crust. While they ate,
Lydia Ardrey asked Susanna a series of questions
about herself; politely probing Susanna's family,
education, career and personal tastes. Susanna
answered warily, trying to give away as little

personal details as possible while apparently answering without a qualm. It was not easy. Lydia's blue eyes took on the quality of laser beams; they seemed to slice through Susanna's mind and reveal her thoughts, layer on layer, a busy honeycomb of mental activity. Susanna grew quite worried; the less she wanted to tell, the more Lydia seemed to guess. Susanna was so afraid of what her eyes might show whenever Lydia mentioned Niall that she looked away each time his name came up until, looking back at Lydia on one occasion, she caught such an amused, quizzical expression in the old lady's eyes that Susanna positively blushed, furious with herself as it dawned on her that her careful avoidance of any discussion of him might be just as revealing as any slip of the tongue.

'Sometimes I hate Niall,' Sîan said as she peeled a peach, unaware of any nuances in the conversation.

'Do you?' Her grandmother looked at Susanna who hurriedly bit into the apple she was eating. 'Coffee, Susanna?' Lydia asked. 'Black or white?'

'Black, please—no sugar. Thank you.' Susanna's voice was mild and polite, she avoided meeting Lydia's gaze.

'He's a cynic,' Sîan said. 'I hate cynics, they're so depressing and dreary, always expecting the worst, always seeing grey skies and no rainbows.'

'A cynic is a disillusioned romantic, isn't he, Susanna?' Lydia asked gently, smiling, but it was Sîan who answered.

'Oh, I hate definitions like that, it reminds me of school and those awful quizzes where the answer is always a trick. Niall believes that everyone is guilty until proved innocent, that's what I mean by a cynic.'

She sounded bitter but then Susanna remembered her own teens; a mournful bitterness went hand in hand with young love and adolescence. Having spoken in a voice like the knell of doom, Sîan languidly ate her glowing, golden-fleshed peach with obvious relish, and smiled at Susanna as she wiped her fingers on her napkin.

'We still haven't heard Susanna's definition,' Lydia pointed out.

'I haven't got one, anyway I hardly know him.' Susanna realised she sounded incoherent.

'When you know him better, I shall ask again,' Lydia said with silent and maddening amusement, her eyes laughing.

'I don't want to know him any better,' Susanna snapped, suddenly losing her temper, and the door opened as if her raised voice had attracted attention. Niall stood there with his girlfriend who was looking disapproving. Susanna got the feeling that the other girl felt she had fallen among people who did not know how to behave.

'What's wrong?' Niall asked, looking from one to the other, his black brows pointedly raised. 'Why the angry voices?'

'You're imagining things, Niall,' Lydia said. 'Good heavens, angry voices indeed! We were discussing something.'

'What?' he asked, looking at Susanna.

'Nothing important,' she said with a heady triumph as she met his eyes and suddenly guessed that he had overheard more than he was admitting. 'Nothing worth bothering about,' she added, somewhat gilding the lily.

Niall pushed his hands into his pockets and looked like a man hanging on to his temper by the skin of his teeth. 'How is the discussion about Sîan's future going? Do you think she has any talent, Miss Howard?'

Ultra polite, Susanna said: 'I'm sure she has, Mr Ardrey—the question is, what does she really want to do?'

He looked grim. 'I see, you haven't got any further than one of these vicious circles.'

'I don't know why you don't send Sîan to one of these wonderful Swiss finishing schools,' said his girlfriend. 'She'd have a super time, terrific fun.'

'I am not going back to school!' Sîan had gone brick red. She glared at Jill, who looked alarmed. 'Don't talk about me as if I was six years old!' Sîan got up and ran out of the room, pushing past Jill as if she wanted to hit her.

'Sîan, come back here!' Niall exploded.

'No, let her go,' Lydia said calmly. 'She's upset.'

'Her manners get worse every day. Why do you encourage her? She thinks she can do just as she likes now that she's left school.' Niall's hard-boned face was constricted with rage, his eyes icy grey, his mouth taut. Susanna looked at him with acute dislike and he caught the stare and looked back with an answering hostility. 'What are you looking at me like that for?' he demanded.

'You big bully,' Susanna said contemptuously, and he seethed; visibly torn between coming over there and wringing her neck, and pretending to ignore her. He compromised by snarling.

'I might have known you'd only make matters worse!'

'You might,' Susanna agreed and Jill looked from one to the other of them, her eyes narrowed and attentive.

'I don't think we've met, have we?' she asked, offering a hand. 'I'm Jill Hardwick.' She smiled with her teeth but not those alert eyes, which were assessing Susanna inch by inch; working out how much her simple green linen dress had cost, how much her low-heeled cream shoes, deciding that her brown hair was dull and ordinary—compared, that was, with sleek black hair and a complexion of magnolia creaminess.

'I'm Susanna Howard.' Angrily amused, Susanna didn't bother to smile and she had already worked out that the white silk blouse and tailored black skirt which the other woman wore had cost as much as Susanna earned in a week. The blouse had top designer written all over it; it had that casual throwaway simplicity.

'I'll go up and talk to Sîan,' Lydia said, gripping the arms of her chair with both hands as she levered herself up with that slow care which spoke of pain if she moved too fast. Susanna watched her, frowning. She must be older than she looked; her face had so few lines and held such sweetness, but the first impression of her was deceptive. What was she? Nearly eighty, Susanna guessed now.

Niall had offered his arm, but Lydia gestured impatiently. 'No, thank you, I can manage—I'm not a helpless invalid, you know.'

'I want to talk to Sîan, too,' Niall insisted, following her out of the room.

Jill gave Susanna a sideways look, leaning over

to pick up a peach from the silver fruit bowl, and beginning to peel it with a tiny silver knife from the table.

'Niall's been having a simply dreadful time with Sîan lately; he's been tearing his hair out, poor darling. She got mixed up with some ghastly fortune hunter.'

Susanna stiffened, watching the other girl's smooth profile. Jill delicately sliced the peach in half and bit into it.

'They're rather sharp,' she said, swallowing the mouthful of fruit and dropping the rest of the peach on a plate. She picked up a napkin and wiped her fingers carefully, talking in a brittle voice meant to be humorous. 'Mind you, I'm always baffled by anyone who gets taken in by those types—they're so obvious! But Sîan isn't very experienced, poor sweet. Too wide-eyed by half! You know how it is when you've been away at school for years—like being in a convent, you can't wait to get out and have some real life. This guy must have had a walk-over. Sîan was probably dying for it, but when she started talking about marrying him Niall almost had a fit.' Jill dropped the napkin over the half-eaten peach, her mouth distasteful. 'But he managed to get rid of the guy, thank heavens. Niall's too shrewd to be taken in by someone like that.' Jill ran the fingertips of one hand over her slim body, looking down. 'I shouldn't eat a scrap! Look at me—I could lose stones!'

'Oh, not *stones*!' Susanna said with angry, saccharine sweetness and had the satisfaction of watching Jill's jaw drop. Of course, she hadn't meant a word of that. She knew she was so slender she was almost on the point of being anorexic, she had been fishing for compliments but she wasn't getting any, not from Susanna, who had listened with mounting rage to those vile comments about Alex. A ghastly fortune hunter? Alex didn't have the right sort of character to be a fortune hunter—he wasn't practical enough or realistic enough. Alex was emotional and unstable; he felt too much and thought too little. Fortune hunters had to be made of tougher stuff. Susanna had known that everything Jill said was a lie and pure nonsense, but that didn't make it any easier to listen to, especially as she was only too well aware of Jill's source for all that insulting rubbish. The only person who could have given her that impression of Alex was Niall, and knowing that that was how Niall had talked about Alex made Susanna's throat burn with bitterness.

'I've seen you somewhere before, haven't I?' Jill asked, frowning.

'Have you?' Susanna was noncommittal.

'We haven't met before?' Jill tapped her regular white teeth with one perfectly manicured fingernail, thinking hard. 'Are you a friend of Lydia's? Do you live in Brighton? Or were you at school with Sîan—is that it?' She was trying to place Susanna, uncover her reason for being here. 'You don't work for Niall, do you?' There was a flash of uneasiness in her eyes, she obviously didn't like the idea of that.

'No to all the questions,' Susanna said with wicked glee, enjoying Jill's irritated expression.

'What do you do? You must have a job.' Jill was inspecting her hands for rings. Susanna caught the disappointment in her eyes as she saw that there was no wedding ring on Susanna's left hand.

'Must I?' Susanna retorted, deliberately awkward. 'How do you know I'm not on welfare? Or I could be Niall's mistress or . . .' She stopped as Niall walked into the room. His grey eyes were riveted on her; he had halted mid-stride, his face reflecting incredulity.

Jill gave a peal of angry laughter. 'What a weird sense of humour!' She turned her back on Susanna, sliding a hand through Niall's arm. 'Can we go, Niall? I really have to get back home before four, remember, to help Mummy. We've got people coming for dinner tonight and there's so much to do.'

'Yes, of course.' Niall looked briefly at Susanna. 'Sîan wants to talk to you—will you go up and see her?' He did not wait for a reply, he left with Jill and Susanna heard the front door close firmly behind them. She was pink and breathless. Had he heard what she was saying? Yes, of course he had, she knew that perfectly well and she had seen that blank, long stare he gave her, before walking out with Jill. What had he been thinking? Well, she knew that, didn't she? He would believe she had been telling Jill that she was his mistress.

Susanna almost stamped up the stairs. Why had she let her irritation with Jill run away with her? Why had she tried to be funny? He already thought that her brother was a fortune hunter. Now he would probably think that *she* had designs on *him*. 'I could kick myself,' she muttered aloud and heard someone laugh.

Looking up in dismay, Susanna saw Lydia looking at her from the landing. 'Why could you kick yourself?' Lydia asked with amusement, and Susanna's flush deepened in embarrassment.

'Oh, nothing,' she mumbled. 'Niall said Sîan wanted to talk to me?'

'Yes, she does—she's in the room on the right.' Lydia looked seriously at her, then. 'Susanna, will you answer one question absolutely honestly?'

Susanna hesitated. 'If I can but I hate being asked that—it usually means I won't want to answer the question at all.'

Lydia smiled involuntarily. 'You're a strange girl. I think you've got what we used to call integrity; nowadays I think they call it being bloody-minded.'

'Niall does,' Susanna said spontaneously and then wished she had not opened her mouth, because Lydia gave her that bright-eyed, attentive look again and Susanna was afraid of her, she saw too much.

'You're a witch,' she said accusingly and Lydia laughed.

'Why, thank you, Susanna, I'm flattered.' She did not ask what Susanna meant which merely went to prove that she was far too perceptive and quick-witted.

'Well, what's the question?' Susanna asked in resignation.

'Do you think Sîan is genuinely in love with your brother?' Lydia watched her face as she asked the question and Susanna sighed.

'I knew it would be a really rotten question. I don't know, Lydia—that's the truth. I simply haven't any idea. And before you ask, I don't know if Alex loves her or not. I'm sure he believed he did, but they're both very immature and over-emotional. I don't think they know what they feel. It's my guess that both of them were looking for something which would make them feel happier. They thought falling in love would do it, so they fell in love, which raises another question—if you deliberately decide to fall in love does that make it any the less real? It seems to me to be like falling off a cliff—whether you jumped or were pushed or just toppled over, does it make any difference once you're actually on your way down?'

Lydia listened with a wrinkled forehead, smiling but intrinsically serious. 'I think I understand what you're saying,' she said slowly. 'You mean that if they think it is real, then it is real, whether it is a genuine love or one they've dreamt up without knowing the difference?'

'Maybe I'm the wrong person to ask,' Susanna said.

'Why should you be?'

'Oh, well, I've never . . .' Susanna stopped, on the point of admitting that she had never been in love herself and met Lydia's sharp blue eyes.

'Yes?' Lydia prompted and Susanna's face burnt.

'Oh, nothing—shall I go in and talk to Sîan, then?'

'Aren't you going to finish that sentence? How maddening of you. I shall die of curiosity now. I wonder what it is that you have never done?' Lydia looked as if she knew; her eyes held mocking amusement which was not unkind, a tender teasing to which Susanna responded with a cross shrug.

'Oh, lots of things, I should think. The things I've never done would fill a large scrapbook. I've never sailed around the world or eaten birds' nest soup or climbed Mount Everest or even ridden on a white elephant—when I come to think of it, I've scarcely done a thing, really.'

Lydia laughed. 'You're very good at that.'

'What?' Susanna asked, smiling.

'Covering your tracks. Go and talk to Sîan.'

Still flushed, Susanna went into the small bedroom Lydia indicated and found Sîan sitting on a pink bedroom chair, her legs crossed in a lotus position, her hands clasping her knees and her eyes shut. She looked like a mournful young Buddha.

'Meditating?' Susanna watched her as Sîan opened her eyes.

'Susanna, Niall just told me that Alex has left the agency, he says Alex resigned, he wasn't fired—is that true?' Sîan sounded angry and upset, her huge blue eyes cloudy with unshed tears.

'Yes, that's true. Alex got another job with an advertising agency, resigned and has gone off to Spain for a holiday before he takes up his new job. He didn't want to work for your brother any more; you can see why.' Susanna's voice faded away as she saw the tears sliding down Sîan face in a fine, glistening track. 'What on earth's the matter, Sîan? Don't cry like that.' She crouched down beside the chair, took out a handkerchief and dried the girl's wet face. 'Ssh . . . stop it now. What's wrong?'

'Alex,' hiccupped Sîan, pushing her hand away. Susanna sighed, but felt sorry for her.

'You mustn't worry about Alex—he has got a much better job, now; earning more money, doing more interesting work.'

'But don't you see? I gave him up because Niall threatened to fire him if I didn't, and I thought Alex might not get another job and his pride would be hurt and Niall wouldn't give me any of my money, he swore I wouldn't get it until I was twenty-five, not a penny, he said, and if I stayed with Alex I'd have to live on what he earned and if he couldn't get another job what would we do? Alex would start to hate me and we'd be miserable and where would we live? I could have learnt to cook properly but I've never had to run a house and it all seemed too much, I couldn't have coped with it, Niall said I'd just make a fool of myself if I tried, and cause Alex a lot of grief in the meantime and he was right, and I hate him.' She put her hands over her face, sobbing violently, like a wild hysterical child, her whole body shuddering with uncontrolled emotion.

Susanna had listened intently. So that was how Niall had persuaded her to give Alex up? He had painted a gloomy picture of their future together if they went on with their marriage plans, and been so convincing that Sîan had given in, flinching from the prospect of ruining Alex's life.

She pulled Sîan's hands down and firmly dried her face again, pushed the hankie into her shaking fingers.

'Blow your nose and don't start crying again, just listen to me. You're blaming your brother because you made the wrong decision—right?'

'Well, Alex has left the agency anyway and he did get another job and it would have been okay if I hadn't let Niall talk me out of it,' Sîan burst out.

Susanna shook her head wryly. 'Personally I think it would have been a disaster.'

Sîan stiffened, looking at her with reproach. 'You agree with Niall! You're on his side! How can you?'

'I'm not on anybody's side, except perhaps Alex's! You hurt Alex by walking out on him with a few words, you know. You didn't give him a chance to tell you how he felt about your brother's threats. You didn't wait to see if Alex was scared or worried, you just left. I'm sorry, Sîan, but I have to tell you this—you're just not mature enough to marry anyone. Alex doesn't need you and I don't want you to hurt him again so stay away from him, will you?'

Sîan clenched the handkerchief in her fingers, her eyes shadowed and dark. Susanna felt angrily sorry for her, but she was afraid that Sîan might try to see Alex again and it would all start up once more. She had to make Sîan see it wouldn't work.

'I'm sorry, but that's how I feel,' she said, walking to the door. Looking back, she added more gently, 'If I were you I'd start thinking things out for myself. You're old enough to have more sense. You're wasting your life at the moment, there are a hundred things you could do, why don't you find out more about cooking or art or anything else you think you might like? It could be fun, and never mind what your brother thinks or wants—he isn't you. He can't live your life for you and if you try to live your life for him, you're crazy.'

Sîan just stared at her and Susanna felt a rough impatience mingled with sympathy as she looked back. The girl was so beautiful, yet frail, like some trembling, heavy-headed flower which could be blown away by the next wind.

'Grow up, Sîan!' Susanna said gruffly and walked out.

CHAPTER SEVEN

SUSANNA spent the next few days working solidly on her redecorating; getting up just after dawn and going to bed well before ten to make sure of a good night's sleep. Her aching muscles demanded it. Even a relaxing soak in a hot bath did not disguise the fact that she was discovering muscles she had never known she had, and each morning when she got up she decided grimly, as she stretched and groaned, that when she got back to London she would make sure she took regular exercise.

One morning a week later she woke up to find autumn had arrived. The air was crisp and cool but bore the scent of apples and dying leaves, a spider had spun fragile cobwebs across the bare branches of the lilac tree outside the kitchen window. Glistening with dew, the elaborate filaments trembled and shone as the wind blew through them, and Susanna ate her breakfast watching them, fascinated by the patterns and their structure. She idly drew one on the back of an old envelope, smiled as she sketched in a big black spider lurking at the edge, then began doodling while she worked out that she would just have time to finish the small bedroom before she had to drive back to London to pick up Alex from Gatwick. There was no phone at the cottage, of course, and if Alex had sent her a card it would have gone to her flat, so she had not heard from him since she left London, but she imagined their arrangement still held. When she did get back she might even find a message from the publisher to say that the Hardy text was ready and she could go ahead with her illustrations.

A blackbird perched on the lilac tree a moment later, lifted his orange beak to the sky, the autumn sun giving his feathers a blue gleam, and sang, his throat bubbling with liquid music while Susanna listened, reluctant to start work yet. The wind still blew quite coldly; the bird's feathers ruffled and he shivered, deciding to move to a warmer spot. Smiling, Susanna looked down at the envelope on which she had been doodling and was taken aback to find she had been unconsciously sketching a caricature of Niall. There were only a few lines but it was enough to make a speaking portrait; there he was, frowning blackly, vibrating with life.

'Damn,' Susanna said, screwing the envelope into a ball and chucking it towards the waste bin. That was what came of sitting about daydreaming; she would be much better off finishing the decorating. She got up, cleared the kitchen table of her few breakfast items and dumped them into the sink to wash up later, then went upstairs. She was wearing her oldest jeans, a light blue shirt, sneakers and a cotton scarf tied around her head, with her hair tucked firmly under it out of the way of any paint drips. She had not bothered to put on any make-up; she did not expect any visitors, and she wanted the minimum of trouble. This week she had kept her mind on work, she had not even had the energy to read the two books by Hardy which she had brought down with her. She had barely had the energy to think, for which she had been rather grateful. When she did think, what her mind came up with disturbed her, as it had worried her just now to find herself drawing Niall Ardrey. He was taboo; a forbidden subject and it was typical of her contrary subconscious that it should insist on dredging his image up at odd hours of the day and night.

She was up a ladder carefully painting the ceiling in the small bedroom, an hour later, when she heard someone downstairs, the sound of the front door closing. Susanna turned her head, stiffening, her paint brush dripping slightly as she listened.

'Hallo? Susanna?'

The deep voice was only too familiar; it wasn't even a shock to hear it because she had half wondered if it would be him the second she heard the first sound. She climbed down the stepladder and put her brush into the metal tray which usually held it when she was not using it, wiped her hands on an old rag and went to the top of the stairs.

Niall was at the foot of them, looking up. The shadowy little corridor gave his features mystery.

'Don't you ever knock?' she asked and he answered quite mildly, half smiling.

'I did but didn't get an answer.'

'Then you should have gone away, not walked in without an invitation. I'm very busy, I have to get my decorating done before Wednesday and I still have a whole room to finish.' She was talking sharply but her eyes were busy absorbing how he looked, startled all over again by the effect he had on her metabolism. He was very casually dressed this morning in jeans and a black shirt which was

open at the throat, giving a glimpse of brown skin
and a rough tangle of black hair. Susanna's throat
closed convulsively, she swallowed, angry with
herself. He was a man, that was all; his body
different in so many ways to her own, not merely
in the most obvious way but in skin texture, body
hair, muscle and shape. Why did she let it get to
her? Her senses seemed to lead a life of their own
these days; far too preoccupied with Niall Ardrey's
masculinity, they refused to calm down even when
the man himself wasn't there. When he was, they
went crazy, and that had to stop.

'Do I come up—or will you come down?' Niall
asked with mockery, a foot on the bottom stair,
and her nerves skidded in alarm at the idea of him
joining her up there, her imagination rapidly
coming up with a scenario which made her cheeks
burn. The door to the main bedroom was open;
she glanced at it before she could stop herself, her
body rioting with a sensuality she fought against,
hurriedly plunging down the stairs without
another word.

Niall smiled as if he guessed what lay behind her
rapid descent and she halted a step above him.
'Well, what do you want?'

His brows lifted quizzically. 'Care to rephrase
that?'

She looked back resentfully. 'Don't play word
games with me, Mr Ardrey. You may have time
for idle chat but I'm busy so say whatever you
came to say and then let me get back to work.'

His smile faded. 'Charm isn't your strong point, is
it?'

'Where you're concerned—no. I wouldn't want it
to be.'

'Don't you like men?' he asked drily, and she gave him another angry look, wishing at the same time that she didn't look so dishevelled; in her oldest clothes and without make-up, her hair tied up in an old scarf.

'They have their uses but I'm not in the market for one at the moment and if I was I certainly wouldn't pick you. You seem to have a very short memory, a convenient one, no doubt. I'm very fond of my brother and I object to the way you talk about him.'

'It may surprise you, but I'm fond of Sîan,' he retorted.

Susanna laughed disbelievingly and his eyes hardened.

'I acted in what I saw as her best interests,' he snapped. 'She's very young and innocent and I want her to be happy. I'm ready to accept that your brother wasn't insincere. Maybe he was in love with her, on his side it was perfectly genuine. I may have been wrong about him. I'm not infallible.'

Susanna's lip curled. 'You don't sound too sure about that.'

His face took on an angry colour, he looked at her with a familiar hostility which she was secretly relieved to see. She had almost been provoking it; it was safer than that other feeling.

'Can't you see it from my angle?' he demanded. 'I may have been hasty in drawing conclusions about your brother, but coming back to find that letter, and Sîan gone, it was the only way to see it. I'm sorry if he got hurt. All I wanted to do was stop Sîan making a mess of her life and I did it as swiftly as possible, I thought I had to act fast or it might be too late.'

'That doesn't explain why you went around telling half the world that Alex was an unscrupulous fortune-hunter,' Susanna accused.

He stared, brows drawn. 'What are you talking about? Half the world? I haven't mentioned it to anyone, it wasn't something I was eager to talk about, I didn't want my sister mixed up in a public scandal. Do you think I'm stupid?'

'Your girlfriend knew.' Susanna did not believe him although he sounded vehement enough.

'Girlfriend?' His eyes were suddenly narrowed, piercing. 'Jill Hardwick?' He surveyed her in silence for a moment, then said: 'She mentioned it to you?' He sounded taken aback and Susanna laughed angrily.

'She seemed delighted by your exploit, she boasted about it at length.'

'Did she realise that you were Alex's sister?'

'I've no idea but from the way she talked about Alex she probably didn't—or if she did she was being deliberately spiteful.' Susanna wouldn't have taken a bet on either interpretation; Jill Hardwick seemed to her to be capable of anything. She might have thought it was a good joke to sneer about Alex to his sister.

Niall turned and walked away but didn't leave the cottage, he went into the kitchen and after a moment's hesitation Susanna followed. He was standing by the window looking at the garden; she saw his gaze resting on the cobwebs which had held her own attention earlier that morning. The dew had melted on them now and they were drooping, blown into ragged disorder by the chill wind. Their owner was busy doing repairs, scuttling along his frail pathways and back again to where he had cocooned an insect in a soft grey blanket until such time as the spider felt in the mood for a snack.

Niall shifted and gave Susanna a wry look. 'You aren't going to believe this but I did not tell Jill anything about what happened. If she knows, someone else told her. At a guess, I'd say it was Sîan. She spent some time with Jill a couple of weeks ago. Lydia wasn't feeling too well and I thought it might be better if Sîan went away.' He gave a faint sigh, frowning. 'Lydia isn't strong; her heart is a problem, we have to watch her carefully. That's why I don't let Sîan spend too much time with her now. Lydia always protests that she can manage, she loves having Sîan, but the truth is Sîan doesn't understand how old her grandmother is. Lydia will be eighty this year, she's not as tough as she'd like everyone to think.'

'She's wonderful,' Susanna said with more warmth, and he smiled at her.

'Yes, she is. She's had a lot of grief in her life, but she has taken it without a whimper. Her husband, my grandfather, died more than forty years ago, but she never remarried although I know she had a number of proposals. Some of her admirers still hang around, without much hope. One of them isn't seventy yet. He once told me that he'd proposed to Lydia every year for a quarter of a century and she always turned him down, very gently; Lydia has enormous tact. She told him she would never love anyone again, she still loved her husband.' Niall's grey eyes were brilliant with affection, his hard bone structure relaxed and full of charm as he smiled.

Susanna was touched. 'How beautiful. I wonder what he was like?' She looked at Niall, unconsciously thinking: like you? Do you take after your grandfather? If he did, she could understand why Lydia refused to consider marrying again.

Niall was watching autumn sunlight trickling down the walls, he wasn't apparently aware of her.

'They had two children—my father and his sister, Alice. Alice died when she was ten, she was drowned in a lake. My father was in the boat with her, it overturned and he wasn't strong enough to save her. Lydia said he had nightmares for years, woke up every night crying, Lydia used to lie awake listening for it so that she could get to him at once. She was a widow by then, it was only a year since her husband had died. The shock must have been appalling, she still has pictures of Alice in her bedroom.'

Susanna listened, horrified, remembering the tranquility she had seen in Lydia's face and wondering at it. How had she managed to cope with two such blows in such a short time, and still smile as though life had been very good to her?

'My father was a haunted man,' Niall said flatly. 'All his life. I didn't know it when I was small, of course—I was frightened of him, he seemed so remote, he wasn't a man who showed his emotions, he didn't know how to. . . .'

'He must have been afraid of loving anyone,' Susanna thought aloud and Niall looked sharply at her.

'Yes, of course, I realised that years later, when Lydia told me about Alice, but I was nearly twenty by then and my father was dead. It was the day after he died that Lydia finally told me. I was shocked when he died but I couldn't feel any grief, I didn't really know him. I was guilty about that and I suppose it showed. Lydia's very quick to pick up things like that, she has amazing intuition where feelings are concerned.'

Susanna looked down, slightly pink as she remembered the shrewd looks Lydia had given her whenever Niall's name came into the conversation. How much had Lydia guessed? The day Susanna visited her she had spent half an hour in the parlour with Lydia after leaving Sîan upstairs. Lydia had talked about Niall for part of the time and Susanna had carefully avoided catching her eye. She had confessed to Lydia how impatient she had been with Sîan and Lydia had gently told her not to worry; Sîan would grow up in her own time. 'It won't hurt her to hear a few home truths, it may even shock her into taking a good look at herself. It seems very natural that you should resent the way your brother has been treated, I'd like to meet him one day.' Susanna had been grateful for the comfort and the support but her frank glance had told Lydia that she didn't want Alex to meet any member of the Ardrey family again, and Lydia had silently accepted that.

'When I was young I almost hated my father,' Niall said quietly, not looking at her, his eyes fixed on the window. 'My parents were never happy together, the house was full of conflict, I used to hear them quarrelling in their bedroom at night and pull the bedclothes over my head to shut it out.'

Susanna held her breath, not daring to move, watching his tense profile with a new feeling; not so much sympathy as anxiety, a changing awareness. She felt like someone used to a black outline who watches intently as it is filled in, shaded with colour, given sharp detail and a new reality.

'It was my father I blamed, of course,' Niall said, his jawline hard. 'He was so cold to me, I never got anywhere near him, and I put my feelings into my mother and took her side instinctively. Children do, I suppose; it is always your mother who is there during the day.' He gave a long, harsh sigh, shrugging, his wide shoulders almost defiant at the memory.

'I just didn't realise,' he went on a moment later in an angry voice. 'My mother was very beautiful, I believed what I saw and she seemed perfect to me, she was very good at keeping up a façade and of course nobody hinted at anything hidden behind it, not to me, not then. It only came out when my father died and she went off to Italy with one of her lovers—Lydia had to tell me the truth about that, too. She didn't tell me much, even then, I had to winkle out the whole story for myself bit by bit over the next few years. It must have started soon after my parents were married. God knows what my father went through. Lydia tried to tell me my mother was sick, it was a neurosis and as she got older it got worse because she was terrified of getting old and losing her looks. Having a new man every couple of months made her feel safe, convinced her that she wasn't like other women, she could keep time at bay. I'm no psychologist, maybe that's the explanation, I don't know and I frankly don't care. All I know is that my father must have gone through hell and all that time I was disliking him and taking my mother's side.' He stopped short and turned suddenly, his eyes fierce.

Susanna almost flinched from that look, it held a demand which made her whole body shudder.

'Do you know why I'm telling you all this?' he asked rawly.

As tense as a coiled spring, she slowly shook her head and Niall's lips curled back from his teeth in a smile like a snarl.

'Nor do I. I've never told anyone. I would have been too sick to let a soul so much as guess and I was very glad then that my mother had been such a damned hypocrite, at least nobody outside the family knew. Even Lydia didn't know all of it. I got some stories from my aunt, my mother's sister, but most of what I discovered I got from my mother's diaries. She kept very full accounts. I read them and I burned them. I stood there for half an hour, watching, until all that was left was ash. She'd taken Sîan to Italy with her. I had to go over there to get Sîan after my mother died. The guy who had been with my mother had already gone, taking half the furniture and all the money my mother had had. Sîan was there with a girl who'd worked in the house. She was a quiet little thing.' He ran a hand over his face as though to expunge some memory. 'I brought her home to Lydia. That was when I found the diaries and a box of old letters, some of them going back years. I needed to know everything or I would have burnt the lot at once. Sometimes I wish I had.'

Susanna had been thinking, watching him intently. 'Was Sîan your father's child?' she asked very softly and Niall looked at her with a wry distaste.

'I asked myself that for a long time. I admit, that was one of the reasons why I didn't get very close to Sîan, I couldn't after reading that diary, every time I saw her I remembered ...'

Poor little Sîan, Susanna thought with sadness.

She could understand the way Niall must have felt at the time, but Sîan had only been a child, it had not been her fault that her mother had been unfaithful to his father.

'But as Sîan grew up she was so much like Lydia,' Niall said. 'The likeness is unmistakable, I couldn't miss it. She's my father's child, no doubt about it, and once I realised that I felt guilty about something else, I shouldn't have kept her at a distance, the way my father did me. I tried to get closer to her, then. I'm very fond of her now, not least because she reminds me so much of Lydia, but I couldn't help wondering if she would ever start to behave like my mother.'

'Oh, no! Sîan? How could you think she ever would? It isn't in her character.' Susanna was appalled again, looking at him with shocked eyes.

He gave her a sombre look. 'You didn't know my mother—she was deceptively sweet, on the surface nothing seemed less likely than that she was a. . . .' He broke off, grimacing. 'Well, that was why I was so angry when Sîan ran off with your brother. I had half expected it once she began to grow up, that was why I was so insistent that she should go to university. I thought it would give her a solid background, make sure she didn't go off the rails. When she bolted with your brother I saw the pattern beginning again and I wasn't going to stand by and let it happen.'

'If you want to find a pattern for Sîan, you must look at your grandmother, not your mother,' Susanna said gently and he nodded.

'You're probably right but the day I got back from New York and found that letter and realised Sîan had gone, I wasn't thinking clearly. I was angry and bitterly afraid. I wanted to break things.'

'I remember,' Susanna said with quiet wryness and their eyes met. Niall relaxed slightly, half smiling.

'You were lucky,' he said. 'In the mood I was in, I was half inclined to break your neck when you kept insisting that Sîan wasn't in your flat. I barely managed to keep my temper.'

'You didn't,' Susanna said. 'You lost it. Very loudly.'

Niall's smile became warmer, less strained, the darkness was fading from his eyes a little although his features were still tense.

'You don't wrap things up, do you?' he murmured, watching her oddly. 'You say it how you see it. Nobody could call you deceptive; you don't hide a thing.'

Don't I? she thought, distinctly worried by that remark. I hope I do. I don't want you guessing anything about me, there is too much I don't want you to know. After all Niall had told her about his family background she might feel she knew him much better and could understand his aggression and the violence which seethed beneath the surface of his face at times, she might even be able to forgive him for the way he had treated Alex, but that did not alter her deep reluctance to let herself care for him, not least because her brother would never forgive her if he found out that she was involved with Niall Ardrey.

He looked her up and down with sudden amusement. 'Go and change. Let me take you out to lunch. I want your advice about Sîan—and this time I'll listen. She doesn't seem able to make up her mind what she wants to do now. I've accepted that she won't be going to university but she must do something.'

Susanna pulled the scarf off and her hair tumbled down in ruffled disorder. 'I really shouldn't stop work or I'll never get the last room decorated before I have to go back to London.' Her voice was uncertain, she wanted to go out to lunch with him, but she knew it wasn't wise.

'Please,' he said coaxingly and she was amazed to hear the difference in his voice, to see the smile in his eyes. It weakened her determination, softened her into an answering smile, although her eyes were still wary because the more she saw of him the more dangerous it became.

She glanced at her watch. 'Well, if I'm back by three I could still get some of that room done this afternoon.' Then she looked down at herself, grimacing. 'But, really, I'm not fit to go anywhere expensive. My hair's a mess and I've got paint under my fingernails, I can't get it out quickly, it will take me a good half an hour to get ready.'

He grinned. 'I'll wait—but don't worry about it. I'm only wearing jeans myself, we wouldn't be able to go anywhere very classy. I thought a pub lunch? There's a good pub in the next village.'

'The Stag? Yes, that's known for its meals.' Susanna cheered up; there was no chance of romantic intimacy at 'The Stag'; it was always crowded at lunchtimes because the man who ran it was popular and his wife produced such delicious bar snacks. People came from miles around to have lunch there and in the evenings it was even more crowded. Susanna and Alex had often driven over there, they knew the landlord and his wife quite well.

'Okay, then, I won't be long,' she told Niall and hurried upstairs. While she was stripping off her paint-stained clothes, taking a hurried bath, scrubbing fiercely at her hands to get the last traces of paint from her skin and from under her nails, her mind kept dwelling on what Niall had told her. Clearly Sîan knew nothing of all that—at least, not consciously, although as she had lived with her mother until she was eight there must be a great deal of unrealised evidence buried inside her mind. Children notice and understand a good deal more than the adults around them realise, and more especially those things that adults do not want them to know. Sîan must have had a simply appalling childhood, poor girl; no wonder she looked so haunted and unsure. Sîan had always said that Niall did not like her; she had known instinctively that he didn't want her around. All Sîan's accusations about Niall's coldness and lack of interest in her had been well-founded, in spite of what Niall had said when Susanna threw them at him soon after they first met. He had tacitly admitted that they were true, now.

Everyone needs to be loved, especially in childhood, and the troubled dark blue of Sîan's eyes gave away her sense of being unloved, her awareness of rejection from her brother and her uncertainty about herself in consequence. Had Sîan half believed that it was her fault that her brother didn't love her? Did that explain her impulsive behaviour with Alex? Lonely, aching for affection, needing to be reassured, Sîan must have grasped eagerly at the first glimpse of a love she had wanted for years without daring to believe she would ever have it.

Niall had said he felt guilty about Sîan; so he should. Yet the way he had behaved had been dictated by his own childhood, his bitterness towards his mother and his guilt because he had never loved his dead father. The way people act isn't always consciously determined; they are formed by what has happened to them in the past and both Niall and Sîan had very troubled backgrounds.

Anyone with any sense would steer clear of both of them. Niall's hard assurance, his fierce manner and overbearing insistence, obviously hid a man who had only ever had one good personal relationship—with his grandmother. Niall had no blueprint on which to base his private life; he had grown up in the centre of an emotional maelstrom, learning that the relationship between a man and a woman can be painful and wounding, and any woman who got involved with him would probably be asking for trouble.

Susanna slid into a towelling robe and padded barefoot into her bedroom to get dressed; her eyes full of anxiety. Was she being wise in agreeing to go to lunch with him? Probably not; yet she felt guilty about talking so bluntly to Sîan last time she saw her and she wanted to help her. Now that she knew so much more about Sîan's family she understood her better and liked her more.

She hadn't brought many clothes with her, not expecting to need much more than a few pairs of jeans. She pulled down a cream sweater and a dark brown pleated skirt. They would be neat but scarcely glamorous, they would do well enough for a pub lunch, especially as the last thing she wanted to do was make Niall notice her. She paused before the dressing-table, staring disapprovingly at her own reflection in the small mirror. Her face was flushed, her eyes too bright— she told herself hurriedly that both facts could be explained by her recent bath and the haste with which she had been getting ready. She looked away and dressed rapidly, then sat down to drag a comb ruthlessly through her hair and put on a little light make-up.

She gave herself a last, quick inspection, frowning. Why had Niall suddenly told her so much about himself? That was what was nagging away at her. He had said he never talked about his private life, he wasn't the type who confides intimate details to anyone, that was something she had instinctively known about him anyway. So why had he told her that long story? Had it been on impulse? Or had he wanted to talk about it after years of locking it all away inside himself? Had it been his guilt over how he had treated Sîan that made him want to explain to Susanna why he had acted the way he had? Had he been excusing himself? In telling her, had he been in a sense excusing himself to himself and using her as a way of absolving his own guilt? He was not what you could call a simple man; far from it, he was as complex as a Chinese puzzle. She suspected that his mind was a shadowy labyrinth, a maze with paths leading in circles, getting you nowhere if you tried to work out their plan. Perhaps he didn't even know much about himself. He had lied to her when he denied Sîan's accusations. Had he told her the truth now? Had he told her all the truth or given her merely a partial glimpse of it?

Sighing, she slowly went down the stairs. Niall

was still in the kitchen. He was sitting by the window reading the book she had left on the table after breakfast. Susanna watched him while he was unaware of her; her eye restlessly skimming over his bent black head, the clear hard profile, the muscular power of his relaxed body. She bit her lip angrily as she felt a savage stab of arousal, her blood running hotly as he shifted and his open shirt showed her the intimate ruffle of curling black hair on his chest. She wanted him, but she did not want what desire could bring if you gave into it. She was afraid of the consequences of a serious relationship with any man, but particularly this one.

Niall looked up, suddenly, and his face altered, a smile came into his eyes and his mouth curved as though seeing her lifted his mood. Susanna's heart stopped and began again with a rush.

'You look very demure,' he said with a glint, running his eyes over her from head to toe. 'Like a nice schoolgirl dressed up to go out with Daddy.'

Susanna pulled herself together and gave him a mocking look. 'Oh, you're not quite that old.' She lifted her brows enquiringly. 'Are you?'

Niall dropped the book and came towards her with a menacing tread but a gleam in those grey eyes that she found distinctly worrying.

'Provocation?' he asked softly.

Susanna decided that discretion was the better part of valour and backed. 'I'll get my jacket. Is it cold?' She was whirling out of the room before he reached her but she heard him laugh and her cheeks were hot when she came back with her jacket on. 'Ready?' she asked, keeping a safe distance.

'I've been ready for a long time,' Niall said and the look in his face made her uncertain exactly what he meant. She decided it would be wiser not to ask and merely smiled politely.

'Then, let's go.'

CHAPTER EIGHT

THEY got to 'The Stag' not long after it had opened and found the bar half empty although a little group of people came in on their heels and more customers arrived not long after them. Susanna sat down at a table in the corner and Niall went to order their food and get some drinks. He returned with a glass of white wine for Susanna and a Guinness for himself, and sat down beside her.

'You were right, they did have Chicken in a Basket on the menu so I ordered that.'

'They usually do, it's one of their most popular meals.' Susanna sipped her drink, watching a young man at the bar. Niall glanced that way, following her gaze, and frowned, studying the man curiously.

'Someone you know?'

'A friend of my brother's, they were at school together.'

'Did you live around here as a child?' Niall shifted, turning towards her, blocking her view of the bar and forcing her to look at him.

'All my life until I went to art school and I've come down here often since although I suppose I ought to sell the cottage, it would make sense, but my mother wanted me to keep it and. . . .' Her voice trailed away and she shrugged.

'Why did she want you to keep it?' He seemed genuinely interested and she began to tell him about her mother's anxiety about Alex and her wish to make sure he had a home to run to if he needed it.

'Alex is much more settled these days, though. When he gets back from Spain I'll ask him how he feels about selling the cottage. I've always been convinced that my mother would want me to share it with him on a fifty-fifty basis. When we sell it I'll split the money with him.' She looked up almost defiantly. 'Alex is very proud, he'll argue about it but it's the only fair thing to do.'

'He means a lot to you,' Niall said quietly.

'He's my brother! Of course he does.' Susanna was flushed and impatient.

'Family relationships don't necessarily work out so well,' he said with a wry twist of the lips and she felt an angry pity for him, realising that he was thinking of his own family.

'Lydia means a lot to you, though, doesn't she?' she reminded more gently and Niall gave her a long, silent look before he nodded.

'What was your mother like?' he asked.

'To look at?'

He smiled. 'In character—was she like you?'

'She worried,' Susanna said. 'My father was always ill, he had a weak chest, he had had tuberculosis as a child and it left him with a tendency to catch colds which hung on for weeks. His lungs were badly scarred, sometimes he got asthma and couldn't breathe. My mother was terrified Alex would show signs of the same sort of problem. So she worried and fussed over him and tried to keep him indoors all winter. It drove him crazy, poor Alex, but he was really very patient with her. I think it would have been too much for me, but she knew I wasn't at risk, I was always the strongest of the two of us. I rarely had anything wrong with me.'

'You were tough even then, were you?' he asked with an amused expression.

The landlady arrived with their food and as she put it on the table gave Susanna a cheerful smile of recognition. 'Hallo, Susie—haven't seen you for a while, how are you? Alex okay?'

'We're both fine, thanks, how are you and Pete?'

'Oh, busy, as usual, thank heavens. Well, enjoy your chicken.' The woman hurried away and Niall looked at Susanna with a grin.

'Susie?' he queried. 'Is that what you're called?'

'No!' she snapped. 'I hate it. I prefer to be called Susanna but Alex has always called me Susie, he does it to annoy me half the time, he knows I don't like it.'

'I can see why—I prefer Susanna myself, it suits you.' He glanced around. 'I haven't had a meal in a pub before,' he confessed.

She gave him a wry look. 'You don't surprise me—it isn't really your sort of setting, is it?'

He looked interested, his head on one side. 'What is, would you say?'

She shrugged. 'Oh, expensive restaurants in London or New York, I suppose. I hadn't given it much thought.' She deliberately tried to give the impression that she never gave him any thought at all but Niall did not seem discouraged by her offhand tone, he was smiling as he watched her.

'What made you want to be an artist?' he asked, taking her aback again.

'Good heavens, what a question! I'm good at

art, I suppose, it was what I wanted to do and I still enjoy my work more than anything else.'

His eyes narrowed. 'More than anything else?'

Susanna was instantly wary, wondering why he looked at her as though she had made some revealing statement. His grey eyes were astute, intelligent, very probing. What was he thinking now?

She looked down, away from that penetrating gaze. 'My work matters,' she said flatly. 'But we didn't come here to talk about me, did we?' Did we? she was wondering. 'We were going to talk about Sîan, you said.' He had made that his excuse for inviting her out to lunch—but had it been a ploy? He hadn't even mentioned Sîan yet.

'We'd better eat the food before it gets cold,' he said evasively and for a few minutes neither of them spoke as they ate the golden fried chicken and the chips served with it in a small wicker basket lined with paper napkins.

'Very good,' Niall decided, pushing his empty basket away as he ate the last chip. 'Coffee? Do they serve it?'

The landlady looked over and Susanna gestured graphically to her, getting a nod and a smile in answer.

'She'll bring it over in a minute,' Susanna told Niall.

'Do you mind if I smoke?'

She shook her head and he lit a slim cigar, a spiral of blue smoke drifting over his head as he exhaled. Watching it, Niall said slowly: 'What am I going to do about Sîan, then? She isn't talking to me much these days, I can't find out what she wants to do because when I raise the subject she gets very quiet and Lydia isn't being much help, either. It was partly her idea that I should talk to you. She took to you when she met you.' He gave her a quick searching look. 'You liked her, didn't you?'

'Very much.' The landlady brought their coffee and Susanna smiled at her as she cleared the remains of their meal from the table. 'It was delicious, as always,' she said and got an answering smile, and a cheerful: 'I'm glad you liked it!'

When they were alone again Susanna said to Niall: 'Sîan did mention that she would like to learn to cook.'

'To what?' he exclaimed incredulously, his voice rising. Other customers looked round at them and Susanna flushed.

'Don't get so excited. There are plenty of courses for domestic science in London, Sîan could train professionally and then get quite a good job. There is a lot more to cooking than simply being able to make a meal. I know she said she wanted to take up art, but she was just talking wildly when she said that, she didn't mean it. Frankly, I don't think she has a very clear idea what she wants to do, but it won't hurt to let her take a domestic science course. It can lead to any number of careers and if she changes her mind later it won't matter, she will have acquired some useful skills.'

Niall seemed speechless. He drank his coffee and smoked his cigar, frowning at the smoke, deep in thought. Susanna finished her own coffee and sat waiting for him to come out of his silence. Niall leaned forward and stubbed out his cigar in the small metal ashtray on the table.

'I'll drive you back,' he said. 'Unless you'd like another drink first?'

Susanna shook her head, getting up. 'I must get back to my decorating, thanks.' Had he come to some decision while he sat there smoking? If he had, he obviously wasn't going to tell her about it. He followed her out of the bar and unlocked his white Jaguar. She climbed into it and he closed the door behind her to walk round and slide in behind the wheel. The engine sprang to life and the car glided out of the car park, slowly made its way down the village street, past the churchyard with its overhanging yews, dark green and shadowy above the mossy gravestones. Susanna's eye moved up from them to the tapering white spire which could be seen from miles around since the village stood on a hill.

Niall did not speak as he drove her back to the cottage. His profile had a brooding fixity, his hands moved firmly on the wheel but she sensed that he was driving on automatic pilot, not even thinking about what he was doing. She did it herself, so accustomed to driving that her mind wandered while her body performed all the necessary functions of controlling the car.

He drew up outside the cottage and turned to look at her, his arm resting on the wheel. 'I barely know you,' he said suddenly and Susanna was startled. It was so obvious—why did it need saying?

'No.'

His mouth was wry at the dryness of her agreement. 'But I feel I do—is that crazy?'

'Yes,' Susanna said, her eyes gently mocking, and he smiled, staring into them. He lifted a hand

and ran his fingertips lightly down the side of her face, following the smooth curve of her cheek, that brooding look coming back into his eyes.

'I think you're honest—blazingly so, almost belligerent with it.' His fingers slid round the curve of her chin as if he was memorising the contours of her face by touch.

'Thank you,' Susanna said, wishing he would stop staring at her mouth. She felt her face flushing slowly, not at what he was saying but at the way he was looking at her.

'Loyal, too—I've got a hunch that whatever that brother of yours did you'd rush to defend him.' His finger brushed her mouth softly and she moved so that it fell away.

'What is this?' she demanded. 'I didn't ask you for a character reference. I must go—you may not have anything better to do, but I have.'

'Susanna,' he murmured and her mouth went dry, her body began to tremble. She fought against the langorous weakness which was keeping her there when every instinct of common sense warned her to get away before she made a disastrous mistake, but she couldn't move, her eyes riveted on his mouth as it whispered her name in that low, husky tone.

'I must go,' she muttered, more to herself than him and Niall's voice was suddenly harsh, seeming to answer what she was thinking rather than what she had said.

'No!' His fingers twisted in her hair, he held her with force as he leaned towards her and took her mouth with a hard urgency that made her lips ache and yet incited the sensuality deep inside her. She finally gave way under the sealike surge running through her, her arms going round his neck and her lips parting hungrily under the demand of his. Niall groaned against her mouth, deepening the kiss. His hands slid down her back and under her sweater, explored upwards until she felt them closing over her breasts, cupping them in a movement of possessive hunger. Her heart beat so fast she felt sick, her flesh was on fire and yet it was liquid, weak with desire.

The thin straps of her slip snapped, Niall's fingers slipped under her bra and she gave a faint cry of painful pleasure, her nipples hard and hot, her breasts aching with passionate sensitivity, so that every light touch made her groan. Niall's kiss drove her head back against the seat, her hair spilling in disorder, tendrils of it against his throat. Susanna needed to touch him, she clamoured for the drug of his body to ease the intense pressure of desire. Her fingers explored the muscled length of his throat, feeling the beat of his blood in the veins below that smooth flesh, sliding down inside his open shirt to where his skin was rough with black coils of hair. Niall took a hoarse intake of air, breathing unsteadily, his head lifting for a second before he bent it again to kiss her throat.

Susanna was struggling to think, trying with a sort of desperation to halt the inexorable tide sweeping her away. She did not want to love him like this; it was too deep, too full of need, this feeling possessing her. It threatened her intrinsic self, the deepest level of her nature, where she was inviolate, untouched, free to exist without the weakness of need. It was at that level that she feared love; aware that it would mean a surrender of her whole life, an engulfing of her heart and mind that she dreaded. She did not want to become the sort of woman her mother had been, living for her husband and her children, barely existing outside their lives, centred on them to the exclusion of all else. She wanted to be herself, to live fully as a human being not merely as a woman for whom love is her whole life. Susanna would not give so much of herself, she preferred the shallows of love. That might mean that you would never know the furthest reaches where the sea ran fiercely, but at least you could never be swept away to drown, you were not asked to give everything you were.

Some men would be happy to live with you on parallel lines; sharing your life without demanding the absolutes of love, but she had known at once that Niall was not one of them. He would want your entire self; and what terrified Susanna more than anything else was the bitter knowledge that she would give him what he demanded and hold nothing back. Niall was a drug to which she was fatally susceptible, if she allowed it she could become addicted, and each kiss, each caress of his lingering hands made it harder for her to deny her own aching desire for him.

With a jagged shock of realisation she felt his hands pushing back her skirt, sliding up her thighs.

She opened her eyes and pushed the intrusive hands away, shaking her head, huskily saying: 'No, no, I won't . . .'

Niall looked at her with eyes clouded with passion, their centres jet black, enormous. He was breathing raggedly, his lips parted, his face darkly flushed, she could see his chest rising and falling rapidly and his bones were tense with frustration.

'You're not taking *me* in the front seat of a car,' Susanna muttered.

Niall looked at her with blank surprise for a second, then his eyes cleared and the tense lines of his face softened into something like tenderness. 'No,' he agreed wryly. 'Sorry, I got carried away. I didn't mean to move that fast, things got out of control.'

'Things like your hands,' Susanna said, tidying herself up with hands that still shook. She pulled down her skirt and turned to open the door, slid her legs out and stood up, hoping she was going to be able to walk steadily.

Niall leaned over. 'Have dinner with me tonight? We've got to talk.'

'We just did and I'm too busy to have dinner with anyone.' Susanna looked at him with grim, realistic eyes. 'Mr Ardrey, maybe it's time for straight talking. I don't want to see you again, I don't want to have an affair with you, you would just complicate my life and I don't need that sort of complication. Please, stay away from me, forget we ever met.'

'Can you?' he asked, watching her intently.

'Very easily,' she lied. 'You'll never even enter my head.'

Niall's mouth twisted. He shifted, put a hand into his pocket and brought out a crumpled piece of paper. Susanna looked at it idly and then became rigid with shock as she realised what it was—the envelope on which she had drawn him and which she had flung at the waste bin in the kitchen that morning.

Niall glanced down at it, smiling mockingly. 'I never even enter your head, you said? Do I really look that fierce?'

Flushed, Susanna shrugged. 'I was doodling, that's all.'

'Doodling?' He gave her a dry look. 'You were thinking about me while you were doing it, then.' He pointed a long index finger at the cobweb she had drawn above the little caricature of him. 'Which of us is the spider and which the fly?' he enquired in that soft, teasing voice.

She gave him a startled look, transfixed, only at that moment seeing any link between the two small drawings. It hadn't even entered her head until that second and she gave Niall an angry stare as she realised how quick he had been to pick up that unconscious association of ideas.

'Very revealing,' he said with maddening amusement. 'Interesting to see how your mind works and what's going on under that calm exterior of yours.'

Her flush deepened. 'You had no right to poke about in my house or keep anything you found! Give that to me!' She bent to snatch it and he jerked it out of reach, pushing it back into his pocket.

'I wouldn't part with it for worlds,' he drawled. 'You threw it away, you obviously didn't want it.'

Susanna straightened, swung round and walked away without another word. She wasn't getting into a tug of war with him over an old envelope. She should have burnt the thing, not left it lying about in the kitchen for him to find and smile over. She didn't want him to know that he had been occupying her thoughts, she hadn't liked the amusement in his face or his quick-witted perception over the link between the two drawings. Why hadn't it dawned on her that she had been thinking of him because she was drawing a spider lurking beside a web which trapped unwary prey? Now that he had pointed it out to her, it was so obvious, but why hadn't she seen it before? It irritated her to realise that her mind led an independent life of its own without her consciousness being aware of what was going on at that deeper level.

She unlocked the front door and walked into the cottage. An envelope lay on the mat. Absent-mindedly she bent and picked it up, carrying it with her into the kitchen and halting as she realised that it was a telegram.

She hurriedly tore it open and went white as she read it. She sat down on a chair, reading the few words again as though hoping that she had made some mistake when she read it the first time.

'What's wrong? What is it?' Niall's voice sounded anxious as he came towards her from the doorway. Susanna had not shut the front door, he had obviously followed her in but she was too upset to be angry, she looked at him with strained anxiety, her fingers crushing the telegram.

'It's Alex—he's been taken to hospital, they think it may be typhoid.'

Niall crouched down beside her and gently removed the telegram from her clasping fingers. He read it quickly and looked up at her, taking her hands and holding them in a firm pressure.

'He must have been well enough to tell them where you are, once there was no reply at the flat.'

She bit her lip. 'Oh, why aren't I on the phone here? I'd have heard hours ago, I could be in Spain by now.' She got up, thinking aloud in a restless, shaky voice. 'I'll have to drive back to London, get my passport and pack, get the next flight to Spain. By the time I get to the airport it will be the evening, there probably won't be another flight until the morning, I'll have to wait all that time before I can see him and find out how serious this is . . . typhoid, is that fatal?' She looked at Niall in agitation. 'I don't know anything about typhoid, how bad is it?'

'It's serious but he's young and healthy, he should be able to fight it off, these days they have some very powerful drugs to use against it. It was sometimes fatal before they discovered antibiotics, but modern medicine has changed that.' Niall looked at his watch. 'My car is faster than yours. I'll drive you to London now. Get your things.'

She looked around the room blankly. 'I don't need anything except my passport and that's in London at my flat.'

Niall took her arm. 'We should get to London in an hour and a half, if we're lucky.'

She was halfway down the garden path before it dawned on her that she was letting him take charge without question. She looked up at him, frowning. 'I can drive my own car, there's no need for you to come all that way—it's kind of you but. . . .'

'You're in no state to drive, you're too upset.' Niall pushed her towards his car. Susanna felt she should protest but she was too taken up with anxiety for Alex, she weakly let him put her into the car and sat staring in front of her, her hands twisting restlessly in her lap.

Niall started the engine and the car shot away, the gravel on the road grating under the tyres.

'He isn't strong,' Susanna said suddenly, her

eyes filling with tears. 'He isn't, you see—he's like
my father, he won't be able to fight it, not if he's
alone. I have to get to him or he'll die.'

Niall looked sideways at her with an odd
expression, his eyes intent, listening to the
tremulous sound of her voice as much as to what
she was saying. He took one hand off the wheel
and laid it comfortingly on her restless fingers.

'You'll get to him. My company have a private
jet, it should be available—while you're collecting
your passport and packing a case I'll get in touch
with our pilot and ask him to be ready to take you
to Spain right away.'

The tears spilled down her white face. 'Thank
you,' she muttered, and his hand tightened on her
fingers.

'Stop crying, this isn't like you! Alex is going to
be okay, and you'll be with him as soon as
humanly possible—you mustn't anticipate the
worst, Susanna. Don't let your imagination run
away with you. He's in good hands, what he needs
now is careful nursing and he'll get it in a
hospital.'

She drew a wrenching breath and opened her
handbag to find a clean handkerchief. 'Sorry,' she
muttered as she rubbed her wet face with it. She
found her compact and repaired her make-up,
eyeing herself in the tiny mirror with distaste. Her
face looked small and crumpled, tear-stained; her
lids were slightly swollen, her nose distinctly pink,
her mouth quivering as she tried to smooth lip
gloss on it.

Niall threw a glance sideways as he sped past a
slower car. 'That's better, you look more normal,'
he said and Susanna gave him a fierce grimace.

'Thanks for nothing. I didn't realise I looked this awful all the time.'

He laughed. 'That's my girl, now I *know* you're back to normal.'

'I am *not* your girl,' Susanna said, dropping her compact back into her bag and snapping it shut.

'We'll discuss that later,' Niall said coolly. 'Just now I'm going to have to do some pretty fancy driving to get us to London quickly, so let me concentrate on the road, there's a good girl.'

'And I'm not a girl,' said Susanna feverishly. 'I'm a woman, and don't be so damned patronising.'

'Oh, well, if having a running row with me will make you feel better, go ahead,' Niall said with resignation. 'You quarrel, darling—I'll drive.'

Susanna glared at him; how dare he be so perceptive? What gave him the right to work out why she was edgy and prickly—come to that what gave him the right to call her darling? She stared at the road, oblivious of the other cars, the villages through which Niall shot at a speed that would have petrified her normally, the golden glory of the autumn trees bending low over the road. Susanna ignored them all while she added up all the other reasons she had for resenting Niall's casual assumption of rights she had never given him. It helped to keep thoughts of Alex at bay, it helped to stop her snarling with frustration and a desperate wish to go even faster, it helped to keep her imagination from dwelling on possibilities she could not bear to consider. While Niall drove with frowning concentration Susanna sat beside him and smouldered like a volcano about to erupt.

CHAPTER NINE

IT was almost eleven o'clock that night before she finally managed to see Alex and even then it was only for a moment and Alex was unaware of her. Her face drawn with anxiety, Susanna watched as he moved restlessly, his fact hot, his lids flickering, his mouth moving as he muttered incoherently and inaudibly while his hands gripped the sheet, relaxed, were flung outwards, and fell back to clench on the sheet again.

'Is he drugged?' she asked the nurse who stood beside her.

'He is being given drugs, of course; we must bring down his temperature, it is very high, that is one of the dangers of typhoid, the strain on the heart can be enormous.' The woman spoke fluent English with a Spanish intonation which was charming. 'But you must not worry, in a week you will see a great improvement. Your brother's case is not alarming the specialist. We caught the disease in an early stage.'

'How did he get it? At the hotel? It's disgraceful that there should be an outbreak of typhoid in a holiday resort—is it an epidemic?'

The nurse put a finger to her lips, frowning. 'You will disturb him ... please, come outside, now.' Her voice rose. 'No! Please, do not kiss him!'

Susanna straightened, gave Alex a last anxious look and walked out into the corridor, her legs shaky under her. Alex looked so ill, despite what the nurse had said; his flushed face had a bruised look, his skin glazed with heat and swollen along the cheekbones. His lips had been cracked and dry, his tongue had kept moistening them. Susanna had felt a dart of terror when she first saw him and she was not reassured by what the nurse had told her.

The hospital was run by nuns whose white-habited figures glided along corridors and up and down stairs, only the faint rattle of their long wooden rosary beads warning of their approach. Susanna stood staring blankly at a statue of the Virgin which occupied a niche in the corridor wall, the calm face seeming to stare back at her. The silence in the hospital made her anxiety more intense, she felt horribly alone.

'There is no epidemic here in town,' the nurse told her quietly, gesturing for her to accompany her along the corridor. 'But there was an outbreak in one of the mountain villages, a fortnight ago. Unfortunately your brother visited it the day after he arrived here, he must have drunk some of the water or perhaps eaten food prepared by someone already suffering from the disease. In some of the more remote areas the water supply is not good, tourists are always warned not to drink the local water if there is any question of danger, but we cannot safeguard against a typhoid carrier. Some people have no outward sign of the disease and yet carry it and can give it to others.'

'How soon will we know if he is going to be okay?' Susanna asked huskily. The nurse padded beside her, her long robes rustling and her rosary swaying as she walked. It was so quiet that Susanna could hear every tiny sound, the building had high ceilings and stone floors which echoed the sound of their footsteps.

They reached the reception area of the hospital, the nurse halted and gave Susanna a soothing smile, her sallow-skinned face framed in a stiff white coif from which a veil flowed to her shoulders.

'It is impossible to say how soon he will start to respond to the antibiotics; a matter of a few days, perhaps. Please, Miss Howard, have no fear for your brother, the disease has been contained, his other symptoms already show signs of improvement and once his temperature comes down he will be well on the way to recovery.' She spoke slowly, obviously searching for the correct words and speaking them with gentle gravity.

'Can I see him tomorrow?'

'Of course. You can visit him at three o'clock in the afternoon. You have found somewhere to stay? If not, perhaps we could. . . .'

'I've been booked into a hotel called The Alhambra,' Susanna said and the nurse nodded, smiling.

'Our best hotel, you will be very comfortable there. I know you are worried, Miss Howard, but try to sleep tonight; perhaps I could get you some sleeping pills to help you? You have had a very tiring day, I am sure. Such a long journey.'

'No, thank you, I don't like taking sleeping pills.' Susanna smiled. 'You've been very kind, thank you.'

'You have some Spanish money for the taxi?'

'I have a car waiting for me,' Susanna said. 'Goodnight, nurse.'

'God be with you,' the nurse said, watching her as she walked out of the main doors of the hospital. Susanna stood outside for a moment, looking towards the parking area, and the car which had brought her to the hospital moved forward and halted beside her. The driver got out and opened the door for Susanna to get into the passenger seat. When he had climbed back behind the wheel Susanna told him to take her to the hotel. His English was only limited; but when she had repeated the name of the hotel twice he nodded and set off at a speed which made her clutch the seat, her face alarmed.

Niall Ardrey had smoothed her path to an extent which made her both deeply grateful and oddly worried. She did not like being under such a heavy obligation to him, although she couldn't deny that she had been relieved to have her journey made so much easier than it would otherwise have been. He had taken her to her flat, and while she was packing a case and hunting for her passport, Niall had got busy on the phone—arranging for his company plane to take her to Spain that evening, making a reservation for her at the best hotel in the small resort where Alex had been staying, ringing a local car firm to order a chauffeur-driven car to meet her at the airport some miles from the little town and drive her wherever she wanted to go.

It had not occurred to Susanna to make such practical arrangements; she had been too anxious about Alex to think very clearly, she had only been intent on getting to her brother as soon as possible. As Niall took her to the airport he had briskly explained the various arrangements he had made and Susanna had been taken aback and overwhelmed.

'I'd come with you but I have an important business appointment tomorrow morning and I can't get away,' he had said, brushing aside her stammered gratitude, and she had been even more startled, her brown eyes wide with surprise.

'I didn't expect you to ... it's very kind—but you've done too much for me already, I'm very grateful, but I shall be fine, I can manage alone.' It had not even entered her head that he might come with her to Spain, the bare suggestion threw her into something approaching panic.

'If you need anything, have any problems, ring my office in London. If I'm not there, my secretary will help.' Niall had given her a printed card with his private number on it. 'Now don't lose that,' he said. 'And don't hesitate to ring if anything's worrying you.'

'Oh, really, I. . . .' Susanna had been reduced to stuttering, her face flushed and uneasy.

'Promise me?' Niall had insisted and she had promised solely to avoid further discussion, but she had no intention of asking him for any further help. She found it distinctly worrying that he had calmly made himself responsible for her, taken over her life as though she was his sister, but as she said goodbye to him before boarding his company's private jet she had not had time to think too much about the feelings seething below the surface of her tense face. She had smiled, said thank you again, and turned to go. Niall had caught her hand and as she looked up, wary and surprised, he had bent and kissed her hard, briefly. Susanna had been free again a second later. She had almost run away, very flushed.

Flying to Spain she had been in a state of

disorientation; too much had happened too soon, she couldn't believe in the reality of anything around her and she was in no state to think about Niall Ardrey or to speculate on his motives for taking charge of her life. The whole journey had been a prolonged nightmare; she had been tense and feverish with anxiety, unable to bear the tension of waiting to get to the hospital and suffering agonies of wild imagination in which Alex died or was already dead when she arrived.

It had been a relief to stand by his bed and actually see him. He was very ill, obviously, but the reality had been so much less terrifying than she had anticipated. She leaned back slackly in her seat, staring out at the lighted windows of cafes and restaurants in the small resort, watching couples wander along the pavements, their arms around each other, passing a hotel whose small garden was lit by coloured lights which gave it a fairground look. The driver turned down to the coast and on their right hand she saw the glitter of the sea under a moonlit sky, the heaving waves stretching far away to the edge of sight. On the other side she saw a line of modern white hotels; their windows brightly lit, neon signs flashing above them. The streets were still full of people although it would soon be midnight, the atmosphere of the resort was gay and busy and it grated on Susanna's nerves.

The car drew up outside The Alhambra, a skyscraper hotel of concrete and glass, and Susanna wearily got out and went into the hotel a few moments later after a difficult discussion with the driver, who spoke almost no English. The receptionist was a sallow-skinned man in his forties; his English was heavily accented but more than adequate. Susanna signed the card he gave her, produced her passport, and was given the key to her room. A porter carried her case and escorted her to the room, making polite conversation in a strong American accent but with a very limited grasp of English.

'You English, okay? Just get in, okay? Sure. How long you here? Hot sun now, very good.'

Susanna gave monosyllabic answers but it didn't seem to matter, she got the feeling she was being given a routine patter which every new arrival got.

She tipped him when he had placed her case on the rack at the foot of the bed and he left her alone. She sank down on the bed and looked around the room; it was modern and beautifully furnished, very spacious, and undoubtedly far more expensive than she would have liked. Niall had booked her into first-class accommodation; her bill was going to be astronomical. It wouldn't have occurred to someone like him that she would have preferred somewhere cheaper, of course. It had been very good of him to go to so much trouble for her, but if she was going to stay here for any length of time she would have to look for a quiet little pension whose rates she could afford.

She got up with reluctance, only now conscious of the ache in her limbs and the throb of pain pressing behind her forehead. She unpacked quickly, stripped off and went into the bathroom to take a warm bath. Half an hour later she was on the edge of sleep, her body heavy, her mind dull, too tired to think.

A telephone rang and she groped her way out of sleep, sat up and fumbled for the phone on the

bedside table, her nerves jumping with fear. Was
Alex worse? Was this the hospital ringing to ask
her to come at once?

'Hallo?' Her voice quivered distinctly although
she tried to steady it.

'Susanna? How are you?' She recognised Niall's
voice at once and her eyes opened fully. It was
broad daylight, she must have slept for hours.

'What time is it?' she asked stupidly, one hand
picking up her watch, to look at it and see the time
before Niall answered.

'Gone nine—you sound sleepy, did you sleep
well? How did Alex look last night? I've spoken to
the hospital this morning, they said he had had a
restless night but was holding his own. They seem
quite satisfied with his progress. They told me you
had seen him but he wasn't conscious.'

'He looked very ill,' Susanna said, rubbing a
hand across her eyes to wake herself up properly.
'But they say he's going to be okay.'

'Good, Sîan has been very upset, she wanted to
come over to Spain too, but I told her to wait a
few days.'

Susanna held the phone away from her ear
and stared at it, stupified. 'She can't come, it
would upset him,' she said angrily. 'Doesn't she
realise. . . .'

'Don't get uptight. She isn't coming. When Alex
is better you could ask him if he would let her visit
him.'

'I don't believe I'm hearing this,' Susanna said,
very flushed. 'It was you who . . . now you're
talking as though. . . .'

'You don't sound well,' Niall said. 'Have you
eaten anything since you left London? Didn't they

feed you on the plane? Your blood sugar is probably low, have a good breakfast and try to get some more rest. Is the hotel comfortable? Your room okay?'

'It's very good, thank you for going to all this trouble, I appreciate it, but. . . .'

'Look after yourself,' he interrupted. 'I must go, this is going to be a hectic day for me. Don't forget, if you need anything you only have to ring my office. I've arranged for the car to be available whenever you need it, you've got their phone number, haven't you?'

'That's another thing,' Susanna said firmly. 'The driver said the bill was to go to you, which is nonsense, I certainly can't let you. . . .'

'Goodbye, Susanna,' Niall said and she distinctly heard him blow a kiss. He sounded as though he was smiling, too.

'Niall!' she said angrily but he had gone, the phone was dead. She replaced it, scowling. She had no intention of using the car firm which was probably very expensive, she could take a taxi if she needed to go anywhere. She didn't want to be in Niall's debt; she was going to insist on repaying him for everything he had done, he was being very kind but her independence prickled at the mere notion of letting him pay her bills for her. He might be very wealthy but Susanna's pride would be injured if she didn't pay her own way. It was maddening to feel both gratitude and resentment; the complicated mesh of emotions made it difficult to know how to react to his kindness especially as she wasn't too sure about his motives.

When she got to the hospital that afternoon

Alex was awake and perfectly rational, he smiled at her as she walked into his small room, looking so much like himself again that she could have cried. His face was no longer stiff and glazed with fever, his hands lay still against the crisp white bedcover, not twisting restlessly as they had been last night.

'Hallo, Susie, how long have you been here? They told me you came last night but I was asleep.' He grimaced. 'I felt rotten all day yesterday, it was my worst day.'

'You looked ill,' Susanna said, sitting down beside his bed, and studying him with enormous relief. 'You look much better today.'

'I feel it—my temperature came down this morning. It was a new drug they were trying, the one they gave me first of all didn't have much of an effect, I gather, but they've got it right now.'

'How long have you been ill? When did it start?'

'Only a couple of days ago—they were damned quick to spot what was wrong with me, I thought I just had a touch of tummy trouble but the doctor the hotel called in made me pull up my shirt so that he could see my tummy. I thought he was crazy, frankly. Spanish doctors! I thought, does he expect to see anything? But there were a few red spots there, right enough, and he said: you've got typhoid. I was knocked silly. Scared stiff.' He grinned defiantly at her. 'Well, anyone would be, typhoid . . . it sounded like a sentence of death to me. He had me in here an hour later and the specialist I saw told me I was lucky the guy I'd seen first of all had been so good at diagnosing. The symptoms can mean anything at first. Catching it early meant I'd have a much better chance although he said it can be cured easily enough these days.'

'They think you got it when you went to some mountain village,' Susanna told him. 'There was an outbreak there a few weeks ago.'

'Was there?' Alex looked irritated. 'I remember the place, it was damned hot and I ate ice-cream all day.'

'Ice-cream?' Susanna said and he stared at her, nodding slowly. 'That may have been how you picked up the infection.'

'I bet it was!' Alex said. 'I'll never eat ice-cream again . . . how did you get here so fast? I asked the hospital to send a telegram but I didn't expect you to come out here. I'm sorry to have given you all this trouble. Did you think I might be dying?' His grin was almost comforting; it was something to joke about now but it hadn't been funny and Susanna gave him a wry look.

'I was worried,' she said, and Alex looked apologetic.

'Sorry, Susie. Trust me to pick up some horrible local bug.'

'Never mind, when I'm not visiting you I can do some sunbathing,' she said lightly.

He smiled, relaxing. 'Where are you staying?' He looked amazed when she told him. 'That place? It's very expensive, couldn't you get in anywhere else?'

'Oh, well, I may move to a little pension when I've had time to look around,' she said evasively. Alex still did not look well enough to be told about Niall Ardrey's involvement in her journey, she decided not mention him or Sîan. The nurse came in a few moments later and told her she must leave, Alex had to rest.

'I'll be back tomorrow,' Susanna promised. 'Anything I can get you?'

The nurse frowned. 'He cannot have any food brought in, you realise? He will not be eating for some days.'

When Susanna left the hospital she took a taxi down to the beach and wandered along the seafront, watching the children splashing at the edge of the blue water, the sunbathers stretched out on the sands, their bodies glistening with suntan oil. It hadn't occurred to her to bring a swimsuit, she must buy one. There was a shop in the hotel where she could get one, but the prices seemed astronomic. She paused in her tracks, staring up a sidestreet into a tiny square, gaudy with striped awnings and stalls crowded with fruit and vegetables. A market! She might get a cheap swimsuit there.

For the next half an hour she soaked up the atmosphere in the market; the rowdy sales talk of the stallholders, the pungent scent of oranges and lemons picked from the trees in local orchards, the locally caught fish sliding about on great blocks of ice on another stall, the racks of cheap dresses, the piles of walnuts which had not been kiln dried and whose flesh was moist and soft, the home-made sweets around which the flies buzzed, the leather boots and strings of cheap, plastic beach shoes.

She managed to buy a very demure swimsuit at a price half that which she would have paid at the Alhambra, and, satisfied, began to walk back to the hotel. Tomorrow she really must look for somewhere else, but tonight she meant to sample the food in the palatial dining room. She was beginning to feel quite hungry, having skipped lunch and only having had a very light breakfast.

She had eaten it on the balcony outside her room looking over the green hotel gardens, with their palms and orange trees and glinting among them the rectangle of bright blue which was the hotel pool.

Now that Alex was going to be okay she felt a trifle stupid about the way she had over-reacted to the news of his illness. She had always told herself that she wouldn't get hysterical over such a thing; it was humiliating to realise that when a crisis did strike she had behaved exactly as her mother had always done whenever Alex caught so much as a cold. Obviously it wasn't so easy to reason yourself out of instinctive reactions learnt at your most impressionable time of life. Love and fear seem to be inextricably linked at some level, she thought, making her way back to the hotel. It wasn't a comforting idea.

She changed into her new swimsuit, went down to the hotel pool and swam for an hour in the impossibly blue water, which was crowded with other hotel guests; while others sat about under striped sunshades sipping drinks brought to them by white-clad waiters from a poolside bar. The heat began to drain out of the vivid sky, Susanna climbed out of the pool and put on the white towelling robe she had found hanging on the inside of her bathroom door. She went back up to her room and had a shower, dried her hair vigorously with a towel and then lay down on her bed for another hour to read a paperback she had bought in the hotel shop. She could not concentrate on it, she was too tired. Her eyelids dropped, the book dropped from her hand and she drifted off to sleep.

She woke when someone tapped on her door. Half asleep she swung off the bed and went over to open the door, expecting to see a maid. It was Niall.

Susanna stared dumbly, not believing her eyes. He gave her a quick, searching look which held anxiety.

'Are you ill? What is it? You're so white.' He moved to hold her as she swayed, her ears full of a roaring which deafened her, and her body lay defencelessly against his.

He picked her up and walked into the room, kicking the door shut behind him. Susanna was icy cold with shock, her heart seemed to beat very slowly as her head lay against Niall's broad shoulder. He carried her to the bed and laid her down, sitting beside her, rubbing her hands and watching her with a frown.

She smiled waveringly, the roaring in her ears subsiding, and the beat of her heart speeding up. 'I was fast asleep when you knocked—I must have got up too fast and turned dizzy.'

'Have you eaten lately?' His cool fingers closed round her wrist, the fingertips pressed into her pulse, but he was looking casually at her skimpily covered body and Susanna was suddenly a scalding pink, the hot colour pouring up her face as she realised that she was naked under the brief white towelling robe. The belt was very loosely tied and the robe gaped open over her breasts. She nervously pulled it together and Niall's black brows lifted mockingly.

'Your heart's behaving very erratically—it was

beating very slowly a moment ago, now it's very fast.'

'It was a shock, opening the door, seeing you—I didn't expect you, what are you doing here?' She was talking rapidly, almost stuttering out the sentences.

'Did you eat any lunch?' Niall asked and she impatiently shook her head.

'I wasn't hungry. I thought you had an important business appointment today?'

'I did, I managed to rush through the discussions by lunchtime. Did you have a good breakfast?'

Her mouth indented. 'Why the obsession with my meals? I had orange juice and coffee and a croissant. You still haven't told me why you're here.'

'How's Alex?'

'Much better, thank you. He's responding to the new drug they're giving him.' She tensed as Niall brushed a damp coil of hair back from her face, his fingers lingering to trail down her cheek.

'You seem to have caught the sun,' he murmured and she looked away from him towards the open window where the dark blue night pressed, breathing softly, like a crouching animal.

'It's getting dark, we'd better put the light on.'

He did not move, but his hand softly caressed her throat and the blue vein under his stroking fingertips pulsed hotly, betraying her agitation. 'Why have you come?' she burst out, shivering. 'Don't tell me that you were worried about Alex, you don't even like him, he's no concern of yours.'

'Anything that matters to you is my concern,' he said and the cool statement took her breath away.

'Can we stop pretending, Susanna?' he murmured, leaning over her with one hand on the other side of her body, his arm barring her from any chance of escape. 'I'm in love with you, and you're well aware of it.'

Her brown eyes darkened, their pupils deep pools of lustrous black, her lips trembled, her breathing was fast and unsteady. She didn't speak because she couldn't, her throat had closed up and her mouth was dry.

'You're not surprised to see me,' Niall said in a low, deep voice. 'You know how I feel, I've made it plain enough. I'm not giving up and I'm not going away.'

'I won't have an affair with you,' Susanna muttered, her eyes lowered.

'I see—marriage or nothing?' he said, laughter in his voice. 'I hadn't expected you to be so conventional.'

'Convention has nothing to do with it! I don't want to marry you, either—I don't want you in my life, in any capacity.' She felt the stiffening of his body but didn't look at him. 'I'm not looking for a lover or a husband. I prefer being single and independent, I'm very happy as I am. I don't want to get involved with you.'

'You're too late, Susanna—you already are involved with me,' Niall said and she looked up, then, shaken, her face betraying her vulnerability. He looked down into her eyes, unsmiling, wry. 'Aren't you?'

She shook her head mutely.

'You aren't in love with me?' he insisted and she swallowed, her eyes moving away again.

'This is a ridiculous conversation, I'm not being

cross-questioned as though I was a witness in a court case.' She tried to sound irritated, derisive.

'Look at me and tell me you aren't in love with me,' he merely said. 'You can't, can you, Susanna? Lies stick in your throat. I'll always know what you're feeling, your eyes give you away even when you won't answer. You're almost brutally direct when you do talk—that's one of the things I love most about you, that straightforward honesty of yours.'

She slackened, giving a long sigh. 'Niall, listen to me—I'm not a domesticated animal. I like being alone for most of the time, I don't want to end up like my mother, living through my family and having no life of my own. I'm selfish, I love my work and I get too absorbed in it to be bothered with the ordinary running of a house. Some women may be blissfully happy cooking and washing their husband's shirts and looking after children, but not me.'

'I have a housekeeper, I'm not asking you to take her job, nor would I dream of suggesting you give up your work. I'll often have to go away on business myself, I'll be at my office all day when I am in London—what on earth do you think I'm asking you to do, go into purdah? You have a weird idea of love; haven't you ever had a love affair before?'

Her eyes slid away and he whistled softly. 'You haven't,' he guessed in a thoughtful voice. 'Well, well, who'd have thought it? You make such sophisticated noises, too.'

'I've had plenty of men friends,' she defended crossly. 'I just don't happen to believe in falling in love; it's a myth like King Arthur, a pretty fairy story but no sane basis for a way of life.' She risked a glance at him and looked down again; she didn't like the gleam in his eye or the amused twist of his mouth. He seemed to be very pleased about something but Susanna didn't want to know what it was.

'You're using the wrong tense,' he mocked. 'That may have been how you felt in the past but you know different now.'

'I have *not* changed my mind!' she insisted.

'It isn't easy to change a fixed idea, is it?' he simply murmured lazily. 'I had a fixed idea about women, too—I thought they were all like my mother and a lot of the women I've met have had a lot in common with her. There are probably women like you, too—I just haven't met any of them or noticed them if I have. It took me a while to admit that you were different and to realise that Sîan wasn't just her mother's child, she was my father's too, and took after Lydia more than anyone else.'

'I'm glad you've realised that, anyway,' Susanna said. 'I'm rather fond of Sîan even though she did hurt my brother badly.'

'She likes you a lot, too,' Niall said. 'And I'm sorry Alex got hurt, Susanna—he isn't what I thought he was, I was wrong there, too. I'm prepared to admit my mistakes and learn from them. Isn't that what makes human beings different from the rest of creation? We can reason ourselves out of tight corners—just as we reasoned ourselves out of the caves we first lived in. If people hadn't been able to change a fixed idea we'd all be cave dwellers today, using stone tools and wearing animal skins.'

'Interesting that you should see yourself as a cave man—that's how I've always seen you! When you burst into my flat that Sunday I was surprised you didn't have a club over your shoulder. You may have changed your mind about Alex—but he certainly hasn't changed his about you. He'll be furious when he finds out that I've been seeing you.'

'You haven't told him yet?'

'He's too ill. I will, when I think he's strong enough.'

'You're being rather illogical, aren't you? You just told me that you hated the idea of living for other people—yet you now say you can't see me because Alex won't like it! Make up your mind.'

'That's different, I can't pretend Alex isn't my brother and I can understand why he hates your guts.'

'I've told Sîan that she can see Alex if she wants to,' Niall said, and she looked at him derisively.

'You've told her she can lead her own life, after all, have you? Well, isn't that big of you? If she can only do what she likes after you've given the go-ahead, how free does that make her? And what if you change your mind later? Do you expect Sîan to change hers too?'

'You awkward-minded little hellcat! I'm trying to build bridges, don't you see that? Are we going to argue all night?' He looked at her impatiently, his eyes glittering. 'I'm going about this the wrong way, aren't I? I know you feel the same way I do, I couldn't be wrong about that. You're just too pigheaded to admit it, and you're prepared to throw away something special because of entrenched ideas you aren't very clear about yourself.

Sîan tells me you told her to grow up. Good advice—why don't you take it yourself? Aren't you mature enough to love someone, is that it? Love should be labelled "For Adults Only"; it's too explosive to be handled by emotional adolescents.'

Susanna had listened with increasing fury, her face burning. 'I happen to cherish my independence, that's all. Why don't you take me seriously for a change?'

'Delighted,' he said with soft menace and his hand was at her belt a second later, deftly untying it before she could stop him. Susanna froze in shock as he stared down at the pale, smooth glimmer of her naked body. She heard him breathing as though he had been running; audibly, harshly. His throat moved as though he swallowed convulsively, then his hand was on her breast and she took a deep breath, shuddering, her face burning and her body icy cold.

She pushed his hand aside and shakily grabbed at the edges of her robe to pull them back together, but Niall swung his body on to the bed, his hands pinioning her upper arms, clamping them at her sides. His head came down, his mouth searching for hers. Susanna kept her lips together, twisting away, writhing under the weight of his body but unable to shift him. He caught her hair and ran his fingers into it, forcing her head round, then kissed her again with a demand that finally got to her. She closed her eyes, a sob of surrender in her throat, and her arms went round his neck, her hands clasping his nape, where the thick black hair clustered above his collar.

Niall's free hand was moving along her flesh in an erotic exploration that made her ache with a tense, spiralling desire which was almost intolerable. The heat inside her seemed to burn through her robe, she was bathed in sweat, trembling violently.

Her left hand moved down Niall's shoulder, fumbled with his shirt, unbuttoning it so that she could touch his bare, cool skin. He shrugged out of his jacket without lifting his mouth from hers, flung it away, pulled his shirt out of his trousers and tossed that after the jacket. It was completely dark now; the moon fitfully illuminated the room, coming and going, like the beam of a distant lighthouse, showing her Niall's eyes, his shoulder, the flat, rough-haired plane of his midriff, a brief glimpse and then darkness again. Neither of them was saying anything, their hands did all the talking. Susanna could hardly breathe; her mouth was too dry, her skin prickled with an intense sensual excitement.

Niall buried his hot face between her breasts, groaning. 'This is what it's all about, Susanna. We don't need words when we've got this,' he whispered, his lips sliding over her aching flesh. 'We could argue in circles and it wouldn't make any difference. I love you, you're my woman, the only one I've ever wanted to call mine. You make me laugh, you make me think. I'm not the same man since I met you. You exploded into my life and restructured everything around me and I'm not going to lose you because I need you, and I think you need me. Whatever you may say, your eyes give that away. I'm far from perfect, I know, but I'll try to build every bridge I can to reach you because where you are is where I want to be.'

'Sex isn't a basis for living,' she said quietly. 'You know it's just a chemical reaction.'

'I'd say it was all in the mind,' Niall said, his mouth around the hard nipple of one breast, his words half stifled. 'I think I had a mental image of the only sort of woman I'd ever want to live with, and you were it, the absolute opposite of my mother. I fell the minute I saw you spitting at me in your flat, so small I could put you in my pocket but ready to fight me all the same. My mother couldn't see a man without flirting with him; you just slapped my face and I loved it.'

'So that's where I made my mistake!' Susanna said with regret. 'I should have flirted with you, that would have got rid of you fast enough. What a pity I didn't know sooner.'

He laughed huskily. 'You see, you make me laugh, too. Sex is only the icing on the cake, Susanna; delicious and tempting but certainly not the essential part of love. We have far more than sex in common.'

She caught her breath as his head slid down her body; her senses led a life of their own and she was worried by what he was doing to excite them.

'Name one thing!' she challenged, hoping to distract him. He had shed the rest of his clothes now and the smooth glide of his bare skin against her own had a distinctly disturbing effect on her. She was afraid of giving in to her own desire for the satisfaction that muscled body promised; she had a sinking suspicion that she could end up craving for him with an addict's abject surrender.

'I just did—a sense of humour.'

'I know I've got one but where's yours?' she said, tugging at his hair to stop what he was doing; his mouth tormented, coaxed, incited and she enjoyed it too much.

Niall raised himself and knelt over her, his knees anchoring her to the bed. Moonlight glinted on his face, showing her the tensely aroused features, the pale eyes, the parted curve of his breathing mouth. She began to tremble at the fixed expression he wore, her heart thudding against her ribs.

'I love you,' he said with an almost sombre insistence. 'Tell me you don't love me and I'll go.'

'That isn't fair,' she half wailed, angry and on the point of tears.

'Tell me. All you have to do is tell the truth.'

'You're making it sound simple, and it isn't, it's very complex. How do I know it would work out, how do I know it will last, that it's even real?'

'This is real,' Niall said, picking up her hand and placing it on his body. Her fingers jerked in shock and she was breathless. involuntarily exploring the sudden descent into the valley of his thighs, the rough tingle of the dark coils of hair. Niall gave a stifled gasp of pleasure.

'I love you,' he said again, and Susanna gave in to the piercing desire which was rising in her again. She lifted her head to meet his mouth, her body arching as his came down to it.

'I love you,' she said at last and he heard it even though the words were half-smothered under his kiss. His arms slid under her, lifting her, holding her tightly as though he never meant to let her go.

Take these 4 best-selling novels FREE

ANNE MATHER
born out of love

VIOLET WINSPEAR
time of the temptress

CHARLOTTE LAMB
man's world

SALLY WENTWORTH
say hello to yesterday

Take these
4 best-selling novels
FREE

Yes! Four sophisticated,
contemporary love stories
by four world-famous
authors of romance
FREE, as your
introduction to the Harlequin Presents
subscription plan. Thrill to *Anne Mather*'s
passionate story BORN OUT OF LOVE, set
in the Caribbean.... Travel to darkest Africa
in *Violet Winspear*'s TIME OF THE TEMPTRESS.... Let
Charlotte Lamb take you to the fascinating world of London's
Fleet Street in MAN'S WORLD .... Discover beautiful Greece in
Sally Wentworth's moving romance SAY HELLO TO YESTERDAY.

 *The very finest in romance fiction*

Harlequin Presents...

Join the millions of avid Harlequin readers all over the
world who delight in the magic of a really exciting novel.
EIGHT great NEW titles published EACH MONTH!
Each month you will get to know exciting, interesting,
true-to-life people .... You'll be swept to distant lands you've
dreamed of visiting .... Intrigue, adventure, romance, and
the destiny of many lives will thrill you through each
Harlequin Presents novel.

Get all the latest books before they're sold out!
As a Harlequin subscriber you actually receive your
personal copies of the latest Presents novels immediately
after they come off the press, so you're sure of getting all
8 each month.

Cancel your subscription whenever you wish!
You don't have to buy any minimum number of books.
Whenever you decide to stop your subscription just let us
know and we'll cancel all further shipments.